DEDICATION

For my fans, my family, and my friends

who keep asking for more –

this final installment is for you.

Foreword: They say to write about what you know and so I did. This work of fiction was created based on real-life accounts of the incredible experiences of an actual "Psychic Circle." The characters are all fictional, but they carry the blended qualities of many of my friends and family. The thoughts and feelings described by the characters in the story are typical psychic teenagers exploring their psychic abilities. I've taken the liberty to embellish just a few of the experiences while adding some much-needed fictional romance.

I know that the paranormal world is a hot topic right now. In this age of enlightenment, "the paranormal" has become more accepted in our society, as shown by the deluge of psychic and ghost shows, including the paranormal topics filling our bookstores, ever since the *Twilight* invasion, *Secret Circle*, and *Vampire Diaries* came into our lives. This is a great opportunity for me to expose young adults to a very real, unexplainable world out there, helping to awaken their spirituality and allow it to grow and unfold. I hope they will take the messages of trust, friendship, and the need for protection from the story and use this knowledge to strengthen their daily lives.   Namaste, Debbie

Disclaimer: Many events in this book are real accounts of psychic phenomena. Some of them can be scary and quite dangerous at times, especially when it is happening to you. If you are a young person that is experiencing the paranormal or any type of psychic phenomenon, it is suggested that you talk to an adult about it so they can help you to safely explore the paranormal world.   ♥ Be safe. Be protected. Be wise. But, most of all, have fun with your psychic discoveries.

KARMA LIKE THIS

THIS

THE PSYCHIC CIRCLE SERIES ~

BOOK THREE

TO Laura,

Best Wishes

for a speedy

recovery ~ ♡Debbie

D. L. COCCHIO

aka D. L. Cocchio

6-13-2024

" a little light

reading to pass

the time "

Genre: YA/ PARANORMAL ROMANCE / FANTASY ROMANCE/ COMING OF AGE

First Printing: MAY 2023
ISBN-13: 97-98375809366

Published by Magic Moon Press, Amazon KDP.
Printed in the United States of America

ACKNOWLEDGMENTS

With special thanks:

♥ To Gary and Jen for all their loving support.

♥ To my awesome beta readers: Maria Audin, Jeannie Chen, Debbie Campoli, JoAnne Vander Wende, and Barbara Zak, whose wonderful ideas and watchful eyes always nudge me in the right direction. I am forever grateful.

♥ To my good friend and writing colleague, Beth Winklemann Glash, whose welcomed guidance was instrumental in keeping me engaged and on my path. I know you are secretly coaching me from heaven now.

♥ I must also thank the original psychic circle -The Unity Circle – for without you, my friends, there would be no story to tell.

♥ To all my fans for loving the story of Rachel, Billy, and Melody, and wanting to know how it all ends. You are my driving force.

Table of Contents

PROLOGUE

"It's a karmic thing," the old witch tells me. "She will forever want what you have. That's the way it's always been in your past lives and will continue to be in your future unless you break the cycle."

Chapter 1

FROZEN

The air surrounding me, full of static, tickles the hairs on my arms as I lay in a prone position on my bed, in my room. Try as I might, I can't move a muscle. I close my eyes tight, wincing at the escalating pain. Tighter and tighter, my body muscles keep constricting to the point of this physical pain. I cannot stifle my moans anymore. Tears are streaming freely from my eyes, down my cheeks, and dribble onto the mattress, soaking my purple sheets.

Mentally, I perform a body check - arms so tight and straight along my side, legs as stiff as a board, head in a vise, chest taut and twisting. Ugh. My worst nightmare is coming true.

My God, Billy, can you hear me? It's Rachel. *Please help.* I plead in my mind, counting on our telepathic bond. Then I wait, hoping silently that he'll respond.

Nothing.

I try to stretch my fingers towards my phone just inches away from my right hand. No luck.

Closing my eyes, I quiet my mind and recall my morning. I can see it in my head. It's the Fourth of July and we were preparing for a barbecue. I was in my room admiring my new pink and purple bikini in my floor-length mirror, and I sat back down on my bed to answer my phone. Melody, who used to be my best friend, was on the line. Our conversation began as normal as can be, but when she started the incessant ranting about wanting her spell book back, I gave her an abrupt "NO"! Well, she went berserk and started humming a loud tune and casting one of her dark spells in retribution. Over the friggin' phone! Melody is used to getting what she wants; when she doesn't, all hell breaks loose.

"OO-roo-a-kee, OO-roo-a-kee, OO-roo-a-kee," Melody's singsong voice serenaded. Then she sang it again and vindictively rattled off a rhyming spell with a hypnotic melody.

> *"This stiffening spell is just for you,*
> *To bind your limbs, so you can't move, too.*
> *I bind you like this until the deed is done.*
> *Until my book comes back, have no more fun.*
> *Stay this way until I say it's through,*
> *No matter what you say or do.*
> *So mote it be."*

Then she flat-out hung up!

At first, my legs stiffened, as my muscles pulled tight. The sensation traveled down my arms and they went rigid. My heart sank. How could she do this to me?

So here I am frozen, lying flat on my mattress in my room, staring at the ceiling, all alone. All I can think about is retaliation, but it's prohibited. She has reduced me to this. Melody breaks the treaty, so she will have to face either banishment or punishment. Her coven and the elders at the store set these rules when she had her last infraction.

I will myself to be strong and lie here as calm as possible because when I attempt to move, the imaginary ropes around me tighten with each attempt, like a Chinese Finger Trap.

Billy, I need you now! I call out with my mind. My boyfriend Billy and I like to communicate telepathically, but he's not responding this time. Pressure builds up in my chest and I send out the burst of energy that's stockpiled in me in one full release, hoping it will power-blast my message to Billy because he's my only hope.

The weirdest thoughts flow through my head like my parents finding me dead in my bed after my lungs tighten and I expel my last breath. Or my legs tighten so much that my bones break, and I'll never be able to walk again. Very morbid thoughts.

I choke out a muffled cry aloud, "Billy, please help..."

So frustrated, I suck in a sharp breath with a simultaneous shudder. After a few more seconds of silence, I finally get a response in my mind.

Rachel, oh my God, what has she done to you?

I respond, *please just come and bring help. Get the Psychic Circle members.*

On my way, he says telepathically.

Tears are cascading down my cheeks, soaking the mattress below. My sinuses fill with mucus and drip, making me choke. The snot is so disgusting; I can't wipe it away. I'm such a mess! But then I hear footsteps bounding up the stairs. At least my hearing is working. My bedroom door flies open and Billy rushes to my side. He cradles my head in his hands as he assesses the situation. I feel his hands move down my arms and the length of my legs. The warmth of his touch, so comforting, reassures me. When I inhale, the light scent of his Axe® body spray calms me. It takes the edge off of things.

"What the hell did Melody do to you?" There's a slight tremor in his voice. Sensing the intense anger in his energy field, it's scaring me. I'm able to see the worry in his caramel eyes, his bangs flopping over one eye as he hangs over me.

Trying to answer, I swallow deeply, but nothing comes out, so I close my tired eyes in frustration. My mouth is dry like it is full of cotton balls. Instead, I form my thoughts in my head. *Mel is such a bitch!* Then, I send him the blow-by-blow description of what she did to me.

Billy nods in acknowledgment. "Don't worry, babe, you'll be okay." Then he kisses the corner of my stiffened lips so gently. I watch as a single tear falls from his eye, and he swipes at it. "She won't get away with it."

The clattering of multiple footsteps advances our way. I spy the army from the corner of my eye. It's the rest of the crew—Jasmine, Sofie, Clarissa, and Deanna pushing toward me. They are all a part of our Psychic Circle group. Thank God, I need them all right now.

Jasmine pushes past the rest of them and comes to the other side of my bed. "The Stiffening Spell," she affirms softly. "I'm familiar with it." She continues placing her hands on either side of my head near my temples and squeezes with her thumbs. Jasmine closes her almond-shaped eyes. Her brows scrunch together, with concentration written all over her face. She is well-versed in Acupressure, a healing technique passed down from her Japanese grandmother, who learned it from her grandmother. Jasmine is their family's youngest healer.

My eyes are the only things that aren't stiff right now. The warm energy emanating from her palms soothes me, penetrating my skin and setting my insides on fire - in a good way. The warmth pulsates as it makes its way around my head and across my shoulders. My head tilts to the side and I find my words again. "I can move my head!" I blurt out as Jasmine stirs from her meditative state.

"Thank you, God!" she says. "Everyone, gather around close, all around the bed. I think we need all of our energy for this." Jasmine purposefully reaches her hands out toward the others. Billy kicks the door shut behind him, while Clarissa, Deanna, and Sofie link hands around my bed. Billy joins in the circle. I notice the glistening tears in both Clarissa and Sofie's eyes, which kicks off the waterworks in me. The rest of my body is still stiff, so I can't even move to blot my eyes. Clarissa seems to understand, grabs a tissue off my nightstand, and then wipes away my tears. *What a friend!*

"I love you guys," I say as she hugs me.

"Back at you," Clarissa whispers, cradling my shoulder.

"We've got work to do," Jasmine tells us as she puts on her serious face. "Sofie, you're at the end of the circle. Please put your right hand on Rachel's arm and I will do the same on this end. The rest of you link hands and complete the circle right around the bed."

My friends have propped up my head using a couple of pillows. Now I have a clear view of the action since I'm unable to turn my head fully from side to side. I notice that someone has tossed a light blanket over me to cover my bikini. Billy smiles at me and nods. *You're going to be okay,* I hear in my head, but I am incapable of smiling back.

Jasmine looks at Sofie. "Hey, I think we need your shamanic expertise now. Since you can move energy, is it possible to draw the negative energy out of her and disperse it?"

Sofie rubs the native turquoise pendant around her neck. "Let's try it." She gets in position. Her wolf's head rattle pokes out of her back pocket. The leather fringe from her vest tickles my forearm, even though it's still stiff. Sofie smooths back her sandy hair as she closes her green eyes. Suddenly, her humming begins, and she mumbles a chant under her breath. Then she pauses and tells the gang, "In your mind, visualize us extracting the negative spell effects from Rachel's body. See it happening."

Warmth permeates my shoulder blades, as the static energy circulates through my body, in on one side and out the other. Faster and faster, it moves around with a dizzying effect. This ritual lasts for about five minutes. Then Sofie breaks the circle and shakes her hands toward the ceiling. I can view the wavy movement of energy flowing through the air, straight from her fingertips. The static sparks twinkle in the air right above us. "Hi-yah!" Sofie shouts as she waves her hands skyward. "Everyone, raise your hands." The group does the motion in sync.

Sensing my body expelling negative energy feels very freeing, like washing the sand off after a day at the seashore. Slow movement can return to my arms with the help of the purging. The circulating blood helps to relax my muscles. It moves lower to my legs, squeezing and relaxing, returning the warmth in slow motion to my lower appendages. Suddenly, I sit up and lean over to my right, wrapping my arms around Jasmine's neck, not wanting to let go.

Billy hovers over us and embraces us both. He leans his cheek against my hair. "God, I was so scared, Rach," he whispers to me. "Somehow, I knew she was going to try something crazy like this."

"You're my hero, Billy," I whisper as I kiss him right on the lips in front of everyone here in the room. A static charge flows through his lips to mine, causing my body to shiver. I pull back a bit and turn toward my friends. A collective "Aww…" echoes around us.

"Thank you, guys. I thought I was a goner." I look from face to face. There's not a dry eye in the house. Sofie brings up the issue that everyone is thinking about as the room gets still. "You know Mel broke the treaty with this stunt, and they will ban her, right? We have to report this to Silver at the store. It is better she finds out now and deals with the aftermath sooner than later."

We all nod in agreement. Earlier this year, Melody tried to orchestrate events to hurt our group with her black magic, and the Witch Council agreed upon the treaty. Envious of the relationship that Billy and I had formed, I guess she felt betrayed. We confided in Silver, the owner of the Psychic Connection - the metaphysical store in town because things were getting out of control. Besides, Silver is in charge of the local coven and likes to maintain peace at all costs. Her anxiety attacks have been escalating, and so she brought it up to the Elders.

Back then, the elders held a meeting and drew up a treaty granting Melody's coven a special spot to practice their witchy stuff—the witch circle site to the West of the store. In return, the coven agreed to stay away from the area to the East of the store known as the Stone Circle. They granted our Psychic Circle access to practice our meditations there, and the meditation groups from the store could use the space, too. Silver warned us she will punish either group if they attempt any retribution. Some serious shit went down that night. All parties have been cooperating until now.

Melody used to be my best friend before Billy entered my life. She let her jealousy of Billy get the best of her. Mel broke all the rules, and I suspect her current boyfriend, Blaine, had everything to do with this—lots of something. When the Elders find out, they will punish her and Blaine.

You know, I'm basically an ordinary sixteen-year-old girl named Rachel Wells with extraordinary talents like telepathy and psychic ability. All I want in life is to have peace and harmony with my friends. Deep down, I have this compelling obligation to save my ex-BFF, Melody Payne, from all of this evil that has entered her life. We were 'best friends for life' before I met Billy Wolfe, and my life certainly is not over. If I can help free her from all of this, that will free me to focus the rest of my energy on my growing relationship with Billy. At least, I need to try.

Chapter 2

THE CIRCLE

We must do something about Melody. She's a menace to society and a very dangerous hazard to the members of our Psychic Circle. She used to be a part of our group until she started doing little sneaky spells on some members. So, the gang voted her out.

Performing that Stiffening Spell was the last straw, so now I've called an emergency meeting of the Psychic Circle group. It's been a few days since the event. I needed some time to recuperate. We are meeting at the stone circle in the woods behind the little new-age shop in town called the Psychic Connection. It's toward the eastern end of the property–the one mentioned in that treaty.

I hurry, taking the shortcut through the woods behind Pompton High School. When I reach the sidewalk, I cross Main Street and continue past the enormous oak tree behind the store. I always touch the bark of the tree when I pass. It must be over a century old and has tremendous energy. I guess I'm a tree-hugger. Walking with my arms swinging and a satisfied smile, I continue down the well-worn dirt path. I notice the grass on either side of it hugs the path as it winds through the woods, allowing only single-file hikers to tread on it. Not far into the woods, I come upon the clearing. My eyes go wide at the sight of this opening into a swept dirt circle surrounded by massive stone benches with upright stone backs. It's an exceptional sight to behold. We didn't make the benches but were told that members of a psychic group did when they first purchased the store in the seventies. I take a step back at the beauty of the whole thing, and can't imagine how they moved the stones without a backhoe or crane. But the story passed down tells that people moved them by hand.

Anyway, the stone seats are impressive. I head over to the biggest one across the circle and brush off the pine needles and leaf debris collected there. Since I'm the first one, I might as well clean it up. After zipping open my backpack, I pull out a small whisk broom and brush off the massive granite seats for the group. The rejuvenating scent of pine smells so clean and fresh.

In the center of the circle sits a flat, rounded stone table of sorts, and I work on clearing it off. *A perfect spot for some incense*, I think aloud. I take out my incense burner and select two sticks — Frankincense and Myrrh. Both are protective incenses, which I feel we need. Before I light them, I produce a large sage bundle and ignite it first with my BIC® lighter. The sage flares up fast and I blow softly to spread the flame. The pleasant scent saturates the air. Once it fades out, I lean forward to blow harder, so the leaves smoke. Then I stand up straight and wave the billowing smoke from the bundle as I circle the stone chairs, reciting my prayer.

"Lord, please cleanse this area of any negativity from the past, the present, and the future," repeating this mantra until I complete one round. Almost instantly, the heaviness lifts from the area, blown away by a short breeze dancing through. I feel a presence behind me and spin around to come face-to-face with Billy.

"Hey," he says as he pulls me to him.

"Hi," I say, but get interrupted by his lips covering mine in one of his warm, wet kisses he knows I love. "Mmm...," I respond. His arms wrap around me in a cocoon of warmth. My lips turn into a smile and I just melt for a few moments, taking it all in.

"Missed you," Billy whispers as he pulls away a bit to gaze at me.

"Me, too." I turn my head as I sense some movement coming toward us on the right.

Sofie Green comes waltzing by, carrying a large burlap sack that jingles with her every step. She exudes calmness with her laid-back mannerisms. Her peasant shirt and cotton shorts, down to her 'Earth Shoe' sandals, scream out 'hippie chick—lost in the sixties', although she's only a few years older than me. That vintage look has made a comeback. She nods and places her bag on one of the stone benches.

Billy and I break our embrace.

An awkward moment.

Sofie pays us no mind as she takes out her candles and sets them up across the stone table, which she uses as an altar.

"Can I add my crystals to the table?" I ask.

"Sure, this Psychic Circle is open to whatever each of us wants to do. It works best if we each contribute to the workings." Sofie watches me as I carry my blue silk pouch over to the altar and arrange one stone next to each of her candles. I figure I will discuss my choices with the group after everyone arrives.

Billy lays his wolf's head knife on the table and takes a seat. I notice the sun is sinking low in the sky. We need to hurry before it gets too dark to see.

The next guest's large gold hoop earrings jingle as she approaches us. It's my buddy, Clarissa Daya. Once, we were told by a gypsy that we were nurses together in another lifetime during the Civil War. One thing we brought with us from our Civil War lifetime was our obsession with herbs, as I mentioned before.

"Hi Chica," Clarissa says in that island singsong as she reaches to hug me and kisses my cheek. "Brought you this." She hands me a sachet of an herbal mixture of Sandalwood, Frankincense, and Myrrh. My favorite. "Mmm...," I say as I hold it to my chest, savoring the aromatic scent. "Thanks."

Deanna Grey is right behind Clarissa. Her Spirit Bear necklace is swinging with each step. She's carrying a small basket containing Animal Totems. This girl is truly knowledgeable about engaging with Spirit Animals. She brings that animal energy with her everywhere she goes. Deanna's the newest member of our group. She is Clarissa's friend.

We all sit on our granite thrones as Sofie lights all the candles around the incense in the center. "Glad everyone could make it," Sofie says. "We are meeting today to help Rachel brainstorm about what to do about Melody."

We all shift uneasily in our seats a bit at that thought. The air charges up at the mention of her name.

I speak up. "You know, it scares me that Mel can have such control over me — over us. Where on Earth is that coming from?" My jaw tightens.

"I imagine it has something to do with Blaine's energy. Since she's been hanging out with him, they've been practicing spells and performing some heavy-duty black magic." Jasmine Lee explains as she sits forward on the edge of her seat.

"But what is her motive?" Clarissa asks. "I just don't get it."

Sofie rises and walks toward the center of the circle. "Whoa, I think we're getting ahead of ourselves. We haven't even opened the circle yet. Just give me five minutes, then you can continue." Everyone shakes their heads in agreement.

"Okay."

Sofie stands with her arms outstretched and begins... "We call upon the heavens and call upon God and the Goddess to open our circle today for love and guidance. We call in the four elements: Earth, Air, Fire, and Water. And we call in the four directions: North, East, South, and West to give us direction and help us plan our actions to help Melody and be safe at the same time."

I stand, "I brought some crystals to help bring in the energies of the Archangels—Blue Topaz for Archangel Michael to protect and defend us in battle." I show them the stone I placed by the blue candle.

"Love it. You know, Archangel Michael is the defender," Deanna interjects.

"Uh-huh." I nod and pick up the green stone by the green candle. Aventurine is for Archangel Gabriel to help in healing.

"And we know him as the healer," Deanna says.

"Here's Citrine for Archangel Uriel. It's for wisdom and guidance." I point to the yellow stone by the yellow candle. "He's my favorite angel."

"Oh, mine too," Jasmine agrees.

"Last is Amethyst for Archangel Zadkiel. He brings the Violet Flame to protect us with love." The stone is purple. "I hope this works." I head back towards my stone seat.

"Thank you," Billy says with a smile. "Angels are always willing to help. All you need to do is ask." I walk past Billy and sit on the other side of him. Then I reach out and squeeze his hand.

Sofie, our shaman, is all business tonight. She picks up her wolf rattle and shakes it around the circle members, stopping at each of us and rattling it in the surrounding air, cleansing the circle. After she makes a full circle around us, she calls out "Hi-yah!", raising her hands and the rattle in the air as if shaking off any terrible energy. "OK. We can continue." The air surrounding us seems to still itself.

"So again, what was Melody's motive?" Clarissa asks.

Now, that's a loaded question.

Chapter 3

THE SPELL BOOK

"You got this one," Sofie says as I look toward her. I take a deep swallow. Well, do you guys remember I told you about the time I emptied Melody's locker for the principal, right after she transferred to that school in the next town?" I glance around the circle at our group; everyone is nodding.

"Yeah, good riddance to bad rubbish!" Billy gives a forced laugh.

"Come on… most of the stuff I got rid of was garbage, but I was so intrigued by the Spell Book with its handwritten notes and journaling that it somehow made its way into my backpack that day." I fidgeted a bit and pulled out the Spell Book.

The people around the circle make a collective "Oooh…" sound.

"You mean you stole it?" Deanna inquires as she leans forward, her feathered dreamcatcher earrings swaying as though they were pendulums.

"More like borrowed it," I continue, my cheeks heating up. "Billy and I tried a few spells out of curiosity. We think they worked and planned on returning the book, but when Melody was so hell-bent on repossessing it, we knew for sure there was something extra special about this one."

"Yeah, and we found out its secret," Billy adds. He leans forward on his stone seat with his elbows on his knees and his hands palm-to-palm. "Show them, Rach."

So, I flip the book over, open the back cover and dramatically peel up the already lifted corner. A folded-up photocopy of a yearbook picture falls out of the hidden pocket. "I saw that someone had written 'He deserved it' across the student's face on the photograph when I originally opened the paper."

"Oh, my God! That's the kid who lost his voice last year, and it never returned. Isn't it?" Clarissa puts her hand over her mouth.

"Yep." So, I show them the words written in tiny print under the photo in Mel's handwriting. "It's a spell to stop gossip."

"Now you have some damaging evidence on her. That's why she wants this book back," Clarissa confirms with a satisfied smile.

Sofie stands up. She's a couple of years older than us and has already graduated. We like to think of her as our voice of reason. "I know you all have reservations about telling this to Silver at the Psychic Connection because she will notify the Elders. The shop is going to ban Mel and Blaine from entering the shop and from performing any magic, but I can't imagine it any other way." She shakes her head and sits down.

Billy's turn. "I say we attempt to handle this on our own, at least try. If we don't succeed, then we'll tell our secret."

Clarissa speaks up, "Why don't you just hand the stupid book back?" She puts her hands out, face-up, mimicking like she's handing something back.

"She can't," Jasmine blurts out. All heads turn her way. She hesitates for a moment, then continues... "Since Mel knows that you've presumably learned her

23

secret by now, she won't tolerate it. Especially with her cohort Blaine pulling the strings, there's bound to be retribution. This guy seems to control her."

Pressure tightens in my chest, and I can feel my anxiety peaking. "I don't think she's sure about that. If we glue the inside back cover down carefully, she will have no idea we opened the flap. I agree with Billy and Clarissa. Let's seal it up and get the darn book back to her somehow. Then we're finished with it." I put my hands on my head to massage my pounding temples and hang my head down so my elbows rest on my knees. I am through with this whole debacle.

Billy reaches over and rubs my neck. He heard me. *What a thoughtful guy.*

"Yes, I say give it back, too," Deanna adds.

"Me too," Jasmine says.

"Ok. I agree too. It is decided. Give it back, but make a photocopy of the whole book first. That way, we still have her secrets. Then glue the back flap together and deliver it. Don't go alone, though. You and Billy do it together," Sofie instructs.

"It is done. So, mote it be." I say as I stand and draw everyone around the table. We hold hands, thank our spiritual helpers, and blow out the candles.

The sky darkens, and we can detect a loud crack of thunder in the distance. The blackened clouds drift in front of the moon, blocking its light.

I'm not so sure the heavens agree with our plan.

Chapter 4

DANGEROUS GAMES

I've been awake since daybreak, assisting my mom with cleaning out the garage this weekend. She thought it would be practical to get rid of some of our old stuff to make way for the car I've been saving up for. It'll also give me added motivation to work harder to save cash more quickly.

"Rachel, please come over here and hold the ladder. I need to reach for the boxes on the top shelf." I drop what I am doing and grab onto the aluminum legs to steady it. Mom reaches for an army green canvas bag and pulls the rope handles down toward her, when some steel pipes slide through the drawstring gap and fly past her, striking the cement floor with a loud crash.

I reach up and stabilize the satchel as it slides down her torso. "Whoa, close call," I yell.

"Thanks, honey," Mom says as she backs down the metal rungs. She opens the fabric bag after setting it down. "Oh look, it's the tent I had from my scout leader days. Remember the fun we had camping?" Memories of Girl Scout camp come flooding back.

"Oh, let's set it up," I say, as I bounce from foot to foot like I'm revisiting the fifth grade.

She nods and I grasp the opposite end of the canvas. Together, we lug the thing and its accessories to the yard to lay it out. The outside bag smells a bit musty, but the tent still smells okay. Within about ten minutes, we have the whole thing set up. We open up the woven chairs and sit down to admire our progress.

I glance up at the beautifully clear sky. *What a perfect summer night it will be for star-gazing!*

"I'm wondering if Jasmine and I can camp out in our backyard later on. It would be so much fun. I know that you have to work tonight, but you can trust us. We'll behave. Promise."

She looks at me for a moment and shakes her head. "Okay, I'm sure you two won't cause any trouble."

I jump up and wrap my arms around my mother for a hug and a kiss. "Woo-hoo! You're the best." Then I run toward the house to find my phone and call Jasmine. The wheels spin in my head as I drum up an ulterior motive for our little outing. It would be a great opportunity for us to try some astral travel. Jasmine and I haven't attempted that together yet. We keep meaning to give it a go but always seem too busy.

The phone sits on the nightstand in my bedroom, precisely where I left it. I snatch it right as it rings. Billy's name blinks on the display.

I am surprised by his call. He was supposed to be working today. "Hi, what's going on?"

"Hey, Rach. I heard you thinking about some astral traveling, and I wanted to talk to you before you contact Jasmine."

"Oh, did you now?"

"Yeah, I would like to be part of it."

"The thing is… we're camping out in Mom's old tent. There's only room for two."

"If you remember, I can travel from my location to connect with you in the ethers. Where'd you want to go?"

"Billy, I haven't even asked her yet."

"Think about it, though. I'm able to help you guys by making the connection stronger."

For a second, I pause. "Well, I want to spy on Mel to see what she is doing. Didn't think you'd be interested."

"What? Why do you need to do that? Are you looking for more trouble? She's not a good person, Rach." I feel the agitation in his voice.

"I need to know what's happening, instead of being surprised - take it or leave it."

A few minutes of silence pass by.

"All right, I'd like to join you two in the astral plane. I will be your anchor should anything go wrong."

I run my hand through my hair. "Let me talk to Jasmine, and I'll fill you in on the details."

"Okay."

* * *

Jasmine shows up on my doorstep at the same time as the pizza guy. I let her in and give the man money for the pie.

"Perfect timing," I say as I lay down the pizza box on the dining table. Jasmine pulls out a chair and sits down, tossing her duffle on the floor. We chat as we devour the pizza, discussing the astral travel plans for our adventure. Jasmine is okay with Billy linking with us. *Phew, I'm glad about that.*

"Hi, Jasmine," Mom says as she flies by the table and grabs a slice of pizza, wraps it in a piece of foil, and slides it into her bag. She pats her bag. "My dinner tonight for work." She kisses me on the cheek. "Have fun tonight, girls." I hand her a Cola can and she's out the door in a flash. This is her crazy, rushed life.

"Bye," Jasmine calls after her.

After dinner, it's an easy clean-up. We head out the back door after grabbing our bags. I switch on the patio lights and we toss our duffels onto the folding camp chairs I opened up beforehand. We spread out our sleeping bags earlier inside the tent. There's even space for a tiny table between us.

I light up the mini-lantern and position it in the middle. Tonight, we will keep the twinkling lights on around the deck when we flip the others off. I double-check the locks on the five-foot white vinyl fence surrounding the yard. Now I feel safe. The night sky is clear, with a blanket of shining stars.

There are no surprises because Jasmine and I have discussed how Billy and I usually travel. She's good with it. We dress in our comfy lounge pants and tee shirts and lay atop our sleeping bags. We continue the plan by quieting our minds, then I reach out to Billy.

Billy… can you hear me? I ask telepathically. It just takes a minute.

Yes, ready when you are.

I grab Jazzy's hand. *Jasmine, can you hear both of us?*

Yes.

Okay, Billy, we are ready for you to lead us.

Great guys, I want you to envision yourself sitting on a park swing in your mind's eye. Give yourself a push with your feet and swing a little higher.

Okay.

Now, when we are at our highest, we imagine ourselves jumping off the swing into the air, just like when we were kids. On the count of three—1-2-3, jump.

The wind blows through my hair as I see myself jumping and reaching into the night sky. Turning to my left, I see Billy beside me and grasp his fingers. On my right, I am linking hands with Jasmine. A huge smile grows on my face.

Is everyone okay? Billy asks us.

We both nod 'yes'.

Next, we need to envision Melody in her parlor—almost everything is black or gray. Picture it

in your mind, set your sights on it, and with the snap of
your fingers, we will be there.

In a snap, all three of us pop into Melody's living room area. Mel and Blaine are circling a medium-sized black cauldron. They don't see us at all. They are in deep conversation while the three of us stand in the shadowy corner, hiding and viewing this scene.

Blaine dips a ladle into the liquid that is swirling in the cauldron. He fills Mel's goblet, then continues to fill his own. He suggests, "Let's sip it together." Melody pulls back and struggles to get loose from his hold.

"No," she says, adamantly. "That stuff tastes like shit. No More." And she shoves his hand away.

"You'll drink it and enjoy it." Blaine pushes the cups to her mouth. He steadies her with his other arm. "It joins us together." He forces her lips open, and the liquid dribbles down her throat. She spits it in his face. "You'll pay for that," he says as he slaps her face. Then he grabs the athame off of the table and holds it against her throat, "NOW, DRINK."

Melody obeys this time, as we cower in the corner watching this hateful display in front of us.

The party's getting rough.

Billy whispers in my ear with a worried tone, "Think of home, immediately." Jasmine hears him too.

We are flying across the sky and back into our sleeping bags in an instant. Billy returns to his bedroom.

So that's how he's controlling her, Jasmine says telepathically.

You're right, Blaine is so evil, I add.

Now we know for sure, Billy interjects. *You don't know what kind of situation you are walking into with astral travel.*

Anything can happen.

Who can feel your presence on the other side?

I think we just dodged a bullet.

Chapter 5

SHOW ME A SIGN

It's a beautiful August day. The bright sun is high in the sky today, casting its rays and warming my back as we make our way toward the picnic area at Greenview Park. Clarissa carries the basket of food and I have the tablecloths in my satchel.

I flip my black and white paisley tablecloth in the air and let it drift out and down to cover the outdoor table. Then I drop to my knees on the seat part to smooth it out with my hands. Clarissa sits down opposite me. Together we empty the picnic basket contents onto the cloth, a foot-long Italian sub sandwich, potato salad, pickles, and two bottles of green tea. I also packed paper plates, napkins, and straws. Clarissa and I have been trying to plan some friend time for the longest time, but we never get the chance. So, this date was very impromptu, jumping at the opportunity.

I position my hands in the center of the table and expand my arms wide to clear a space in the middle. I am careful not to spill over the food. In that two-by-two area, I spread a blue bandana out and lay my deck of Universal-Waite Tarot Cards on top, along with my two huge quartz crystals. Clarissa and I both used to practice reading the Tarot with each other often, but our time together has become less and less. Life got in the way. Well, today we made some time for each other.

So, we start our little picnic with the food, biting into the sub and savoring every bite. The potato salad is pretty darn good for the store-bought kind. I'm a pickle person too. I believe every sandwich deserves a pickle.

After we're done, I push my plate aside and hold the Tarot deck between my two palms, enjoying the energy emanating from them. They once belonged to my grandmother and the edges of my cards are dingy and worn from all the years of use. I can still feel Granny's energy when I touch them.

"Clarissa, I want to do a three-card spread because I've had this unsettling feeling for the past few weeks like something bad is coming my way. Can you help me interpret them?"

"Most definitely."

I shuffle the deck and cut it several times until it feels right. Then I lay them down in three piles by cutting the stack into thirds. Next, I turn over the uppermost card in each pile. The top three cards revealed are the 3 of swords, 7 of swords, and 8 of swords.

I pick up and hold one of my quartz stones to help boost my energy, asking aloud that the symbols show me what is best for all concerned.

Clarissa points to the first card - the 3 of Swords - which depicts a heart pierced by three swords and she states, "This conveys that the outcome disheartens you."

"Yes, I agree. I'm pretty sure it has to do with the Melody problem. She used to be my best friend."

She points to the 7 of Swords - which depicts a man stealing swords from the people in the background. You know, people tend to take advantage of you and your good nature. Pay attention to this and try not to let it happen."

"Uh-huh." My palms are getting sweaty now.

Clarissa picks up the last card–the 8 of Swords. "When I gaze at this card, my eyes focus solely on the girl tied with ropes and 8 swords surrounding her. Sometimes the first thing your eyes focus on is the true meaning of the card in that reading."

"Is that me?" I ask and point at the girl.

She shakes her head. Yes, I feel you will be bound. Honestly, I mean, someone may actually tie you up or restrain you if you are not careful."

I stare into her eyes. "You're kidding, right?" I say, half laughing.

"Let me pull one more for clarification." Clarissa pulls the next card and flips it over. It is No. 15–The Devil. "This one signifies the thing you do that winds up being your downfall. So, what is it that causes you trouble all the time?" The wind is getting stronger, causing the cards to shift in the spread before us.

I wring my hands in my lap. "I'm told that my fault is that I am always too nice, too caring, and too trusting. That always gets me into trouble."

"Uh-huh," Clarissa agrees.

"Well, I don't think I am going to get tied up with ropes or chains. That's something you see in the movies. Perhaps it just means that somebody will block me or stop me."

I guess I will have to be extra careful in everything I do.

And stop watching horror films!

Chapter 6

LUCID DREAMING

I glance over at my alarm clock, shielding my eyes from the dazzling 3:00 AM shining back at me. I've hardly slept a wink. Dreams have infiltrated my sleep on and off all night, but I can't remember what I was dreaming about. Usually, I remember my dreams vividly. I try pulling up my sheets and fluffing up my pillow to help will myself back to sleep.

That's weird. I grab the edges of the blanket as my mattress suddenly vibrates. My eyes blink wide open to reveal a figure about 5'8" or so at the foot of my bed. He looks very familiar to me with his spiked blonde hair, blue eyes, and warmest smile. It's Melody's father,

Mr. Payne, who passed away last year. He has visited me once before. I smile at him. But I have to confess: I am not afraid anymore.

"Hello, Rachel," he greets me without his lips even moving.

"Hi, Mr. Payne." I prop myself up on my elbows to see him better. He looks so casual in his jeans and Rolling Stones tee shirt.

The man walks around the side of my bed and extends his palms to me. I instinctively slide my hands into his, and immediately I am taken on a wild journey in my mind. He's showing me snippets of Melody and me as Native American friends. A past life. We are holding hands and skipping through the fields, the fringe on our dresses dancing in the breeze as we run. The deer grazing near us comforts me. Happy times. This scene suddenly changes to Billy and I embracing in the same lifetime. I get the distinct feeling we were married back then.

"But, what...," I start to ask. Mr. Payne holds up his hand as if to signify to hold on for a moment.

He shows me the teepee display again with Melody and Billy under some deer skins, getting down to business if you know what I mean. I am right across from them, hidden by the tent flap. In the opposite corner, I spot another person spying on them. A young boy looking very sad. He's wearing a leather loincloth and a beaded headband. I am drawn to his dark, soulful brown eyes. Mel is glancing over her shoulder at him. It seems like she's trying hard to make him jealous. A heavy, crushing feeling in the pit of my stomach washes over me. Being an empath, I can feel all those emotions - jealousy and sadness, secondhand.

The last time this spirit visited me was before the July barbecue. I had a déjà vu during the visit. I realized the boy opposite me was Billy's friend from the gym— Jimmy Lang. Evidently, he's been in love with Melody and has been for centuries. I don't know how, but I know it.

So this is where Jimmy fits in!

Then the scene changes and a different boy is wrapping Melody in a tight bear hug. Her arms are flailing and her fists pounding him. She is not okay with this, and she is obviously struggling to get free. I can hear his message loud and clear, "She's mine and her powers are all mine too." Just like before, I recognize him. It's Blaine, minus all the black eyeliner and piercings.

"Save Melody from this awful karmic cycle. Get her away from Blaine. Jimmy is the solution." I hear Mr. Payne's message very clearly. He had to get through to me because, apparently, I wasn't listening and wasn't acting fast enough.

The vision is the same as before. I think with a little more urgency. I let Mr. Payne's hands slip out of mine, and I slump backward against my pillow as he steps away from the bed.

"Help her soon. Time is of the essence." He takes two more paces back into the shadows and the apparition dissipates.

Dumbfounded, I slip down between the sheets, the static charge from his energy still tingling in my hands. He's never been so urgent in his plea.

I guess we'll have to figure out how to get Jimmy involved in this mess and pray that he will be open to it. Jimmy is the key to this.

Can we actually change a karmic cycle?

Chapter 7

CIRCLE OF STONES

Of course, I am up at the crack of dawn. With fresh memories of last night's visitation, I think I should reach out to Sofie to brainstorm for some important research. She has such a vast wealth of knowledge and probably can help me.

She picks up the call when I speed-dial her. I don't even pause for her to say a word. "Hi Sofie, wait until you hear who visited me last night!"

"Melody?" she responds.

"No, Mr. Payne, her father." I unconsciously twirl my finger in my hair.

"What? He's passed. I need details," she shoots back.

The visit of Mr. Payne remains in my mind, along with all the details. I recount the highlights of my night to Sofie.

"You know what... a past-life regression with Jimmy might do the trick," Sofie blurts out with excitement. "I hope he is open to it. Maybe tonight, if we can pull it off. I'll talk to Deanna since she has that Lakota background, and she has the natural ability to work with animal energy. I understand she has gone through many past-life regressions already.

"You've got it," I say, as my heart drums in my chest. "I'll gather the others. Talk to you later." I hang up my phone and dwell on the subject with a budding ear-to-ear grin.

Now we're getting somewhere.

* * *

At the Psychic Connection, the class schedule is free for tonight, and Sofie persuaded Silver, the store owner, to allow us to have an unplanned Past-Life Meditation session in the lower-level meeting room.

A light pitter-patter against the slate walkway announces the rain's approach. It wasn't supposed to start for a few hours, but here it is a little early in time to set the mood for this evening's event.

Sofie and I are already at the shop, rearranging the area. I grab the next folding chair stacked against the wall and unfold it, placing them about 1 foot apart, then continue making a small ring around the room. Meanwhile, Sofie is setting up a little table in the center of the chairs and drapes a fringed cloth across it. She places her tools on top of the tablecloth—some loose sage, her wolf rattle, and a handmade drum that she uses in her drumming circle. The last thing she adds is an abalone shell containing a tiny bundle of braided sage and sweet grass inside it. She lays her lighter down alongside it.

"Hey, Rach, I need your help with this," Sofie says, beckoning me over to the closet. When she opens it, a large wooden chest at the bottom grabs my attention. The ornate box, adorned with intricate Native American carvings on its side, has a large feather carved into the top of the wood.

"Wow!" I am filled with admiration. "That's so beautiful. Is it yours?"

"Yes, thanks. I did the carvings myself in a ritual workshop with a few friends that were interested in Native American customs. Come, help me drag it out."

We haul the box out of the closet and into the area. It is heavier than it looks. The thing weighs a ton.

"That's far enough. We can open it right here." Sofie lifts the lid and locks the bar in place to hold it open.

My stare intensifies. "What a collection!" I say, marveling at the vast assortment of stones inside. I pick up a turquoise that is the size of an egg. It fits perfectly in the palm of my hand. I take a moment to close my eyes and rub the smooth surface with my thumb. A warm feeling emanates from the stone in my hand and courses up my forearm and upper arm, and across my shoulder blades. Then it pulses down the other arm to my right hand. I suck in a deep breath and blow it out slowly. Wow!

"Turquoise is one of my favorites. I can tell you like that one too," Sofie says as she pats my shoulder. "Put that stone on your chair for you to use later. It will help you go into the regression easier."

"Thanks. That's great. Where do you want the other stones?"

"Help me by gathering the stones and placing one on each seat. Then we'll create a large circle with the remaining gems. Spread them out–they don't need to touch. We want them to empower us with their energy as we go on our past-life journey tonight." Sofie grabs several stones and begins putting them in their places.

Within 5 minutes, we create a beautiful stone circle around the room, surrounding our chairs. Per Sofie's request, I placed one stone on each chair. And I spread out a few more rocks on the central table.

Sofie closes the lid to the carved box and places a turtle shell on the top. I watch as she visits the bookshelf in the room's corner to select a jar of herbs next to the books. She opens it and scoops a handful of the herb inside, then traces the stone circle with a sprinkling of these herbs alongside the stones.

"What's that for?" Curiosity killed the cat.

"It's powdered Sage for extra protection while we are in our meditative trance; it will keep us safe," Sofie explains as she caps the jar and returns it to its place. "One can never be too careful."

We both turn at what sounds like a herd of elephants bounding down the steps into the room. The group has arrived. First is Deanna, holding her Lakota staff out in front of her body. I hold out my hand and brush against her fur-trimmed vest as she walks by me. A handmade fur pouch hangs from her shoulder, and a silver and turquoise bracelet hugs her upper arm. Her short brown hair matches her dark eyes. "Hi," I say to her. Deanna high-fives Sofie as she passes by.

Following Deanna is her best friend, Jasmine. Jasmine is the one who originally brought Deanna to our group. Jasmine wears a silk brocade headband I remember her grandmother had sent it from Japan as her birthday present last year. She treasures that gift. It looks wonderful tied in her short, dark, wavy hair. She is sporting her signature black hooded cloak over her shoulders. "Hi, Rachel. How about a hug?" She reaches over to embrace me.

"Hey."

Sofie tells them, "Sit wherever you want. When you're settled, please grab and hold the stone that was placed on your chair. Someone already took the turquoise, but select the rock that calls to you."

"Aye, Amiga." That's my friend Clarissa. I hug her and bury my face in her curly black hair. Her Herbal Essence shampoo always smells so good. Clarissa has been in my class since the 6th grade.

But it seems like forever. We have discovered we were sisters in a past life and often joke that she's my sister from another mister. Sharing our love of herbs and natural magic, was part of our talents revealed when we were both nurses during the Civil War. When there wasn't enough medicine to go around, we mixed herbal concoctions to help the soldiers heal and fight the pain. A funny thing is that we usually hear Clarissa before we see her, as her gold hoops and bangle bracelets always announce her arrival. Today, she is wearing her famous black tee shirt with the Puerto Rican flag emblazoned across her chest. We clap high and low. I know it's corny, but that's what we do. Clarissa chooses the chair next to me.

Billy is the last to arrive and has his friend Jimmy in tow. Billy sashays up to me, slips an arm around my waist, and plants a big one on my lips. He steps back a little and flips his chestnut hair back from his eyes. He has that cute 'Bieber look' before it went bad. "Hey, I brought Jimmy. We worked out together at the gym earlier today." He steps back and Jimmy leans forward.

"Hi, Rachel," he puts out his hand and I shake it. "Good to see you again."

"Same here."

Billy and Jimmy sit down on the other side of me.

Meanwhile, Sofie flips on a Native American CD, softly playing in the background. The music fills the air with flutes, drums, and chanting. Very soothing.

We pause for a moment and hold the stones that chose us. Sofie thinks the stone energies will calm us down to make the meditation process a little easier. A wave of calmness ripples through my body like my experience with the stone earlier, as I take a deep breath to center myself.

After that, Sofie shakes her rattle to get our attention. We take the cue and are ready to work with her. All except Deanna, who looks like she is out cold. Sofie goes over to Deanna to access the situation and tries nudging her, but no response.

What have we gotten ourselves into?

Chapter 8

BRINGING UP THE PAST

Sofie cautiously slides her hands onto Deanna's shoulders and gives her a little shake. "Come on, Deanna. Time to come back to us."

Deanna's shoulders remain slumped over. Her eyes twitch ever so slightly, remaining in a trance. The atmosphere in the room switches and fear hangs in the air. We each rise from our seats until Sofie calls out "NO," at which point we slide back into our chairs simultaneously. "Stay where you are and let me handle it," she adds. Her panicked countenance is enough for me.

Sofie springs into action and grabs for her wolf rattle. Slowly, she sings along with the rhythmic native chanting in the music surrounding us. Then she rattles her tool above, below, and around Deanna, moving the energy she gathers off her and, in one swift movement, casts it into the ethers. The rattle comes my way as she drops it into my lap, so she can work her magic with her hands. Holding Sofie's rattle upright with both hands, I stare in amazement as it emits static charges from the top of the instrument into the air.

Our young shaman uses her hands, swaying to move the energy around, starting at Deanna's head and expeditiously running down her hair to her shoulders, arms, and hands. Then sweeping down past her hips, thighs, and legs—ending at her feet. We all watch intently as Deanna's eyes flutter the moment Sofie places her thumbs and forefingers on each side of Deanna's temples. Sofie leans over to whisper in her ear. As she speaks her message, she moves her thumbs in tiny circular motions, pressing at the temples, which gets Deanna to open her eyes more. A frightened expression crosses her face. Sofie lets go and embraces Deanna in an enormous hug.

"God, you had us worried," I call out.

"Deanna, what happened?" Billy blurts out.

Sofie holds up her hands in a stop-motion. "Just give her a minute, guys." So we wait until Deanna gets her bearings.

"Can I have some water?" Deanna asks in a soft voice. She pushes her bangs back off her face.

I take a bottle off the table and give it to her.

"Thanks."

A few minutes later, Deanna tells us she fell into a trance immediately after holding her stone. She opens her hand to show a huge quartz crystal point. Quartz intensifies whatever you are feeling or trying to accomplish. The Native American chanting and music almost instantly made her return to a past life. "I was at a Native American Tribal Council meeting. Taking part in the ritual as an elder at the meeting, I couldn't answer when I heard all of your voices. I guess I was stuck in that loop until Sofie broke me out of it. Thank you, Sofie." Deanna explains.

Sofie nods her head toward her.

"Holy crap! Is this something that could happen to everyone? Can we get stuck in the past?" Jimmy asks. He is not so sure he wants to do this now.

Sofie sits down in her chair. "If we each team up with a partner, we should be safe. Hold hands and go under together. You can rely on each other to get you back."

"Maybe since Deanna has done a past life regression several times before, her body automatically knew what to do. She went under so fast." Jasmine adds. Others nod in agreement.

"Well, if you guys want to continue, we can. If not, we will call it quits," Sofie offers. "It's up to you."

"I'm still in," I say.

"Me too," Billy adds as he looks toward Jimmy with a shrug.

"Yeah, I'm in too, I guess," Jimmy shrugs his shoulders in reply.

Jasmine and Deanna nod. "Me too."

"Okay, let's get on with this," Sofie says as she goes around the circle to group us in pairs. She pushes my chair closer to Billy and scoots Jimmy's chair next to him. "You three will be together because we have an odd number. Hold hands," Sofie instructs and then moves on to link Jasmine and Deanna together. Finally, Sofie moves her chair close to Clarissa so they can work together.

Sofie cues the music with her remote and then turns the volume lower to speak above it. "We can all focus on the same period if we set our scene and purpose. We wish to regress to a moment in our pasts when we were Lakota Indians inhabiting teepees. If we can picture it, then perhaps we can re-live it together."

Billy and I hold hands and Billy links with Jimmy. We relax in our chairs with our eyes closed. I hear faint chanting coming from Billy as he sings along with the music. I join in, too. What the heck, let's make this authentic, right? Jimmy joins us. The entire room chimes in.

My muscles relax on their own as the melody of the music soothes me. Sofie is drumming along with the CD. After a short time, the drumming stops. I am so relaxed and at ease that I don't care.

I look up to see that we are all in a circle sitting cross-legged on a grass clearing. There's a fire pit in the center of the ring. A roaring fire is throwing warmth my way. It's like we are in a dream state, but I am truly taking part in this event. Billy and Jimmy are on each side of me, all staring at the fire, as an elder reaches past us and tosses some herbs on the blaze. The flames lick them up. The man is saying some sort of prayer in his native language, but can't make out what he is saying.

Billy squeezes my hand, and as I glance down at it, the fringed leather garments on our arms flutter in the breeze. Jimmy is wearing the same. Across the circle, Sofie, Clarissa, Jasmine, and Deanna glance in our direction. Behind them, an older, dark-haired teenage girl crosses over to a teepee in the background. Jimmy appears to be mesmerized as his hand tightens in mine and his eyes follow her movements. The girl turns momentarily and throws Jimmy a kiss, then stoops down to enter the teepee. A warm and tingly feeling spreads across my hand. And empathically, I can feel the deep-seated love he has for her. Could this be Melody? The maiden has dark hair and eyes, but not Mel's usual dark eye makeup and gothic look. Then again, gothic make-up is a current trend, not in this past life. I try to get Jimmy's attention, but he's not paying me any mind.

The Elder with the long gray braids points to Billy, and gestures for him to come forward. Billy rises and walks over to the man, who then whispers in his ear while he motions for Billy to go back over in the teepee's direction, back by the tree line.

Again, the Elder reappears next to the fire and throws more herbs on the flames as he chants. It makes me sleepy. I can feel my eyelids droop down. When I open them, I am on my knees near the teepee, this time with Jimmy's hand in mine. He's kneeling next to me, and together we pick up the edge of the rawhide material to peek inside.

Just like in my earlier vision–there is a movement under the deerskin blankets inside. Two arms push the edge down to reveal that girl, who I now know is our Melody, feverishly kissing a guy. When she moves her head to the side, Billy's head emerges, kissing her back. My heart plummets. Dammit. How many times do I have to watch it?

Feeling Jimmy's erratic heartbeat pounding next to me has me concerned as Mel turns to look up at us with a sly grin and then assaults Billy with another aggressive kiss. It's turning my stomach.

In my mind's eye, I can see a snippet of Mel around the age of ten holding hands with 10-year-old Jimmy, both in Lakota attire, promising to love each other forever. It's another vision. The next moment, the scene changes again, just like my vision with Mr. Payne. It's not Billy anymore. The scene morphs into a different guy embracing Melody in a tight bear hug in a wooded clearing. His arms hold her so tightly that she cannot break free. This is in modern times. Melody struggles to get free, and he squeezes even tighter. "You're hurting me!" she screams. "Help!"

I recognize Blaine, like before. I hear in my mind - "She's mine this time and her power is all mine, too". There is nothing you can do. He reveals a wicked grin.

The anger bubbling up inside Jimmy, right beside me, shifts from his arm down to mine. My breathing labors as beads of sweat form across my forehead. I feel like I am on fire. I think we're about to blow from the pressure.

"Over my dead body," Jimmy screams out as he pushes his angry energy at Blaine, knocking him over, and causing him to lose his grip on Melody

Suddenly, the world around me turns to darkness, and my eyelids slowly flutter open and close. We are back in the meeting room at the Psychic Connection. Jimmy's death grip is cutting off the circulation in my hand. I yank it back. "Ow."

Jimmy jumps out of his chair and paces behind us. "Over my dead body," he growls out.

Chapter 9

A GRAND PLAN

I sprint down the main corridor, swinging the corner wide, and practically slide through the door to homeroom as the bell rings. Close call. Honestly, I need to make more of an effort to get to school at least five minutes earlier because, for the last 5 days, I've barely made it in time.

Billy gives me a wave from the opposite end of the room as I slip into my desk chair. *Perfect, you made it.* I hear as if Billy is speaking to me, but he's far away in the classroom.

I nod my head and smile at him. *I know*, I answer back. He grins that dreamy smile that I fell in love with.

The early announcements begin with the usual early matter—date, weather, and lunch choices for the day. Then they proceed to more interesting topics. "Now, here's an important message," our Student President says. "As you all know, we've been dealing with the pandemic sickness for almost three years now. The virus that started in China has spread around the world. Our classes were held online to make things safer for our students and faculty. Those that were sick were quarantined at home. When the schools were open again, we all came back to school wearing masks. We weren't able to hold large gatherings, so we haven't had a school prom during this time. Here in the United States, we are near the end of the pandemic and the restrictions for large gatherings are now being lifted."

He clears his throat and rattles some papers before he continues, "This year, we are doing something different and are opting for a Junior/Senior Ball instead of a prom. The theme is 'A Midsummer Night's Dream Costume Ball.' Please sign up if you want to be on the committee and attend the first meeting today at 3 pm in the cafeteria."

The murmurs in the classroom escalate with everyone's excitement. Our homeroom teacher, Mr. Giancola gives us ten minutes to chat about it since he can't compete with the elevated noise. I make my way over to Billy's desk.

"What do you think?" I ask, approaching him.

"Cool idea. I like it." Billy grabs my hands. "Will you be my date to the Ball?"

"Of course," I answer shyly and pull my hand away. Everybody is watching me side-eyed and I hate the attention. I'm going to the group meeting to help plan it. You interested?"

He shakes his head from side to side. "I'm not a committee-type guy. Ask Jasmine or Clarissa. They'll make better party planners. Yes, to the date, but not the planning."

"OK," I say in a disappointed tone.

Billy pats his knee. "Come on, sit here."

"No, not here in school," I whisper. I don't know why he is being very PDA for the last couple of weeks. What's got into him? It makes me very nervous.

Mr. Giancola claps to gain our attention. "Okay, you've had a few minutes to discuss this event. I want you to know that I have volunteered to chaperone. I'm looking forward to it. Now back to school time. The bell will sound to announce the first period any moment now. Gather your belongings and be prepared to go."

I run out the door to see if I can catch the girls near their lockers. As I approach my locker, I spot Clarissa running toward me. She stops inches in front of me and puts her hands on my shoulders. "You want to…" She takes a deep inhale to catch her breath.

I already know what her question is. "Yes, I do," I blurt out.

Jasmine comes up from behind us and shouts out, "Me too! I swear our minds have a definite link. Many times, we have completed each other's sentences. We just have that special connection. Holding hands, we do our little happy dance, like the old 'Ring Around the Rosie' with a few additional jumps and skips. *I know, very corny*.

We try to compose ourselves as we grab our books and move on to our first class.

"So cool."

"Can't wait."

"See you guys after school."

Then we part ways. The rest of the day speeds by.

* * *

At a quarter to three, I close my locker with my homework in my pack and stride fast to the cafeteria to attend the Costume Ball Planning Committee meeting. I sashay in and select a seat in the front row. Clarissa and Jasmine are right beside me. I feel so giddy like the time I found out I made the cheering squad. I guess I need this little excitement in my life to distract me from the situation with Melody.

With a pile of notebooks, papers, and brochures threatening to tumble from her arms, Mrs. Shone, our Phys-Ed Teacher, hurries into the room, stops short, and lets the tower drop onto the nearest table. We jump up to help her by gathering the stuff into a couple of neat piles. "Thanks, girls. I appreciate it."

"No problem," we say in harmony.

Roughly nine or ten other students enter the room, and we shift our seats to form a semicircle near the first table. Mrs. Shone hands out a composition book and a pen to everyone present. "We need to brainstorm some ideas. You can take some notes as inspiration. She smooths down her tunic and pushes her short, mousy-brown hair behind her ears. Mrs. Shone goes for the all-natural look, never wears make-up, and is very plain-Jane, almost boyish in appearance. The gym teachers here are like that. She rummages through her pile of things on the table and pulls out a pamphlet. "This is what I was looking for. Management already approved this venue after we presented our top three choices. I think this is the one that suits our needs best. The teacher holds open the leaflet in front of us.

"Oh my gosh, it's Venetian Village. I went to a wedding there once," says Amanda, a petite, blonde-haired girl from my homeroom.

"That place is gorgeous. My Auntie had my cousin's baby shower there. The food was delicious, and we had a wonderful time," Clarissa calls out.

"I have enough brochures to give you each one," Mrs. Shone announces as she passes around the attendance list. "Please sign in and I will hand you a brochure."

As soon as I get mine, I flip it over and check out the page of photos. This place is something else. It's just perfect.

"So, the primary structure resembles a castle. Then there are several other buildings and alleyways surrounding that building. Behind the key building, there is a stunning ornamental garden with an enormous fountain. We fell in love with it when we saw it." Mrs. Shone puts her arm around Miss Kidd's shoulders the moment she joins us.

"Yes, we did," confirms Miss Kidd. "Hello, people. Glad you could come today to assist us in planning this event. What we would like you to do is to be part of the process of coming up with some ideas for decorations and set design. She reaches up and smooths her hair back into a ponytail. Then she snatches a Sharpie marker from the stand and throws it in my direction. "Heads up. Will you be my note-taker?" she asks. "What's your name?"

"I'm Rachel, and yes, I'll take notes." I never get picked for anything. It's my lucky day. I rush up to the easel.

"The beautiful garden out back reminds me of the play - A Midsummer Night's Dream. Let's think along those lines and let the ideas flow. I am envisioning a woodsy fantasy or a fairytale evening. Any suggestions?" Miss Kidd puts it out there for us.

"How about some Grecian arches, whimsical trees, and some roses?" Jasmine suggests with enthusiasm. I write that all on the easel pad.

"Nice." Mrs. Shone likes the idea. "What else?" The room is full of energy.

"How about those little glittery fairy lights strung throughout the garden? We can string them in the branches. And maybe incorporate some elves, fairies, and sprites in between the plants. It's like a fairytale," Clarissa adds.

"Oh, I have something too," I call out. "The inside should match the outside. So, what if we take some tulle fabric, and drape it from the corners and sides of the room to the center, resembling a tent? We ought to include some more of those tiny lights for a fantasy look."

"I appreciate where this is going," Miss Kidd says with a huge grin.

I am writing so fast that my wrist hurts.

A boy at the end of the row chimes in, "How about creating a picket gate leading to the garden? And a double swing would be a great place for photos. With more of those lights, of course."

The group is sitting on the edge of their seats, leaning forward. I flip the page and continue writing.

"The students will need some ideas of what to wear," I add. "And what they shouldn't show up in."

Miss Kidd taps her lips with her index finger as she thinks aloud, "Okay, let's think Grecian goddess, flowing dresses, flower wreaths."

"Oh, how about accessories like cuff bracelets, fairies, wings, elves, ram's horn headdresses, crowns, tiaras, and masks?" Jasmine asks.

"Yes, yes…" Clarissa is bouncing in her seat. "With gowns we see at the Renaissance Fair, or even steam-punk since it is all fantasy."

Mrs. Shone chimes in, "But the boys must wear shirts–no bare chests, no shorts. Respectful length dresses or gowns. No mini-skirts."

My penmanship is getting sloppy now. Writing fast is not my strong suit. I flip the page again and turn around. "What about a color scheme?" I ask, "Do we need one?"

"Well, since we are in a forest or garden setting, how about greens and browns–earthy colors?" Jasmine suggests. "With a splash of color-gold and purples. That reminds me of a forest fantasy."

"I like that," I say as I write the notes on the page.

"Oh, and the centerpieces could be floating candles on a moss runner across green tablecloths," Clarissa exclaims.

"I love it all," Mrs. Shone adds. "Copy these suggestions down in your books, if you haven't already. We have something to start with. The Theater Department might help with some trees, background, and scenery."

"Awesome brain-storming." I raise my voice and high-five Clarissa. "This is going to be just perfect."

Chapter 10

YES, TO THE DRESS!

I bolt to my locker to gather my books, then dash over to catch Clarissa before she takes off. It's 3:00 pm on Friday and the halls are overflowing with students. Everyone is conversing about the masquerade ball.

Clarissa sees me. "Hi, Chica!" she calls out as I approach her.

I tap my hand on her shoulder. "Hey, what are you doing after dinner tonight?" I shake the flyer about the Midsummer Night's Dream Costume Ball that they passed out today. "I'm thinking of dress shopping."

"Count me in!" she yells. "You want me to ask Jasmine?"

"Yes, but let's keep it at us 3, okay? Too many people mean too many opinions.

"Sound's good."

"Come by the house around 7."

"You got it."

I pat her back and run down the hallway. My excitement about this event is overwhelming. It's difficult to imagine that I've never been to an event you'd wear a gown to, like a ball, dance, or prom. After I push open the hefty metal front door of the school, it bangs against the brick facade. I run to my mother's Honda Civic, fling open the back door, and throw my backpack and jacket on the seat. Then I slide into the passenger seat next to Mom. The whole vehicle smells wonderful from that sandalwood oil that she likes to put on.

"Wow, Rachel, you seem so happy. What is making you so bouncy and bubbly? What's going on?"

I show Mom the flyer. "This is the dance I mentioned. They are calling it 'A Ball.' All my friends are going and they want to shop for dresses tonight. Can I go? Please?"

Mom gives me her usual smirk. "Maybe. Who's driving?"

"Well, that's the thing. It was my idea... so I hoped you would take us. I know I should've asked you first. But do you think you might be able to drive us to the mall?" I put on my best angelic smile.

She shifts the car into gear, and we drive away from the curb. "Rachel, you know I always need some lead time for your shopping excursions."

"But Mom, I made the plans in the heat of the moment. We were so caught up in planning that I couldn't help myself. Can you just drop us off and let me borrow your credit card?" I plead, staring her down.

She turns to stare at me after we pull into the driveway. "What? Oh no, honey. If I am driving, I am coming to the store with you. And my credit card doesn't leave my hand. That's the deal–take it or leave it."

I sigh, fold my arms across my chest, and sit back in the seat. "You know, Katie Jones has her own credit card. Why can't I get one?" I pout.

My mother opens the driver's side door and grabs her purse. "I told you the terms... take it or leave it." She slams her door shut and proceeds up the brick walkway to the front entrance.

I gather my things and run up behind her. I have to play this cool, or I don't buy a dress. "Okay, you're right, Mom. Sorry, I accept your terms. Thank you for saying you'll bring us. The girls will arrive at 7 pm. I love you, Mom." I wrap my arms around her middle and kiss her cheek. We enter the house and figure out what's for dinner.

* * *

At exactly 7 pm., Clarissa rings the bell, bouncing up and down on my front steps. I approach the window and peek out to see Jasmine right behind her. Unlocking the screen door, I push the frame wide open. Both girls grab my hands and pull me onto the stoop. We jump around in a circle like little kids as we sing our mantra, "We're going to the Ball, we're going to the Ball. Woo-hoo!" You'd think we won the lottery.

After a ten-minute drive, Mom takes the exit for Willowbrook Mall, pulls into the parking lot for Macy's, and parks the car. It's Macy's first to see if we get lucky. We race for the entrance and head straight for the escalator to the prom dress section.

My mother locates a bench along the wall and makes herself comfortable. "What kind of gowns are you looking for? Like what style or what color? Tell me so I can help."

Clarissa turns to my mom, "Well, at the planning meeting today, Miss Kidd told us to think: Grecian goddess, cuff bracelets, fairies, wings, elves, crowns, tiaras, flowing dresses, and flower wreaths."

"Like fantasy dresses. Masks are optional." I add.

"We can consider some Steam Punk, which is fantasy, also," Jasmine calls over her shoulder.

"Okay," says Mom, "I know what Grecian and fantasy looks are, but I can't help you with the Steam Punk stuff."

"No worries, Mom."

"How about colors?" Mom asks.

"We're looking for browns, greens, golds, and purples. But I guess any color will work," I tell her.

Each of us is sifting through a different collection, searching for the perfect dress.

Mom speaks up, "How about you each start with 1 or 2 dresses, then we'll move on from there."

"Okay, Mrs. W."

Clarissa pulls a gorgeous light green gown off the rack. Scarf-like layers cascade across the middle of it. It reminds me of something a fairy might wear. "Oh-my-God, will you look at this? I think I've found the one!"

"It's so beautiful," I reach out to touch the fabric.

"Hold it up to your chest," Mom says. Clarissa holds it up and looks in the mirror to her right. "It's stunning.

Let me keep it for you and you can search for a second dress."

"Nope. I only want this one." Clarissa stands strong.

"Okay. Whatever you want." Mom concedes.

I've been searching the rack, but nothing is appealing to me.

Jasmine pulls out a golden Grecian-style gown that crisscrosses across the bodice. "Oh, guys, check this out." She holds it up and smooths down the tulle fabric.

"I love it," I say.

"Nice one," Clarissa checks in.

"I think I'll try on this dress and the white one, too." Jasmine drapes them over her arm.

"How about you, Rachel?" Mom approaches me. "Nothing yet?"

I shake my head 'no', with an exaggerated frown on my face.

She sees me considering a purple satin gown with a black bodice. It has some metal hardware accents across the back, front, and around the waist, with leather straps that circle the upper arms. "Why don't you try it on? That color has always looked nice on you."

"All right, let's do it," I answer as I extract the dress from the rack.

We each enter the dressing rooms, while my mother hovers out by the mirrors to be our judge.

"How about we come out altogether? Ready, one, two, and three..." I part the curtain and we all step out in front of the mirrors at once.

"Oh, girls, you all are breathtaking." Mom holds her hands to her chest. Her blue eyes are already tearing up. Mom has always been sensitive. You should see her watching a Hallmark movie - waterworks, every time.

Our first picks are the best. Clarissa's light green fairy gown fits her figure perfectly. It holds 'the girls' tight against her upper body. "This is the one," she says. We all nod in agreement.

Jasmine tries on the golden dress first.

"That suits you to a tee," I point at her.

"You're right," she remarks with a thumbs up. "Sold!"

I spin around in my awesome purple and black gown. I don't even know what to call it– Steam Punk? It has so many metal accents. "This is perfect," I whisper. I can see Mom is in full tear mode. She is nodding.

"It is exquisite," Clarissa calls out.

"Billy will love it," Jasmine adds.

Standing in a model pose in front of the big trifold mirror, I turn from side to side. Then, I take a deep breath and shout, "I say yes to the dress!" I'm blown away by my appearance. It makes my heart flutter.

Hopefully, it will make Billy's heart flutter too!

Chapter 11

MAGIC IN THE BAG

The heat on my skin causes me to stroke the spot on my arm, stirring me awake. I open one eye to see the golden stream of light caressing my forearm as it squeezes through the crack in the blinds on my bedroom window. It feels so comforting. I rub again and smile. Lifting my head, I glance at the alarm clock on my nightstand. The numbers are flashing at 10:00 am. That's late for me, despite it being Saturday. Hesitantly, I drift back down and shut my eyes, savoring the warmth and quiet.

Good morning, Babe, I hear in my mind. This is my boyfriend, Billy, and I cherish his considerate, telepathic greetings. It puts me in a cheerful mood.

Hey there to you, I respond in my head. *What's going on?*

Thought we might meet with Jimmy as soon as possible. He's been having vivid dreams ever since the Past Life session that we did and he wants to share it with the group, Billy says.

Okay. Just you and me, or the entire group?

All of us. Call me when you're done with your shower.

Will do. I spring up and rummage around for a shirt, then grab my jeans off of the chair. On my trek to the bathroom, I grab my underwear from the top drawer of my dresser. Continuing, I reach over to hang my clothes on the other side of the door and twist on the tap before stepping into the stream of water.

The coldness on my shoulders wakes me up the rest of the way. I can't wait for the water to warm up, since I am so eager to hear about Jimmy having more dreams that could hold clues about how we should proceed with the whole Melody situation. This is so exciting!

I finish my shower, get dressed, and reach for my phone before I plop down in my purple bean bag chair. I push the call button and Billy picks up right away.

"Hey," he says.

"Hey yourself."

"Jimmy will join us at the lake where we did the crystal ceremony."

"Sounds great," I respond. "What time should I tell the others?"

"Like around 2:00."

"Cool. See you guys then," I hang up and call Clarissa and Jasmine. They are going to come and will hunt down Deanna and Sofie.

I run a comb through my hair, brush my teeth, and descend the stairs toward the kitchen. Hitting the button on the coffeemaker, I slide over to retrieve two Pop-Tarts® and pop them into the toaster. What an awesome name for these pastries. The inventor was a genius.

Coffee is ready. I stir in two sugars and cream. Yum. I bring my plate and cup out to the garden, then sit in the lawn chair to enjoy my meal. There's a little nip in the air. I love it. What a glorious day! I haven't been this upbeat in a while. It must be the prospect of getting some clues from Jimmy's visions. Maybe then we'll be able to figure out a solution to our problem - our Melody problem.

My favorite Black-Eyed Peas song—I Gotta Feeling, rings out from my back pocket. It's old school, but I don't care because it makes me happy. I slip my phone out and tap the button. "Hi, Clarissa, I am so excited about this afternoon," I say.

"Me too! I wanted to tell you that Sofie and Deanna can come. Sofie says to bring our crystals. It will help us connect much easier."

"Okay, I like that suggestion," I tell her. "I have an idea, too. Melody's always a risk, so I'm bringing some materials to help create something for protection. You'll see."

"All right. Sounds good. Be there at 2."

I lay my phone down, take a swig of my coffee and thoroughly enjoy my Pop-Tart®. After breakfast, I search for the supplies needed for the surprise that I have planned for the Psychic Circle. Thumbing through some of my mother's books, I discovered something that will be of help to us. It's a recipe for making a Gris-Gris Bag from a book called "Magic's in the Bag." I thumb to page 183 for the ingredients we'll need.

As I gather the herbs from our basement stash, I check them off—black pepper, cayenne, lotus, rue, sulfur. I carefully pour some of each item into individual plastic baggies and label them with markers. It also calls for salt. Got it. Check.

When I hit the next ingredient - what the... where am I going to find barnacles? That's the stuff that grows on the dock and boats down the shore. Uh, oh... may have to abort the mission.

Then I have an "ah-ha" moment. I run up the stairs to my room and snatch the athame from my desk. I drag an empty shoebox from the closet. Carrying the box under my arm, I scurry down the steps and out the sliding door. Along the darkness of the roof overhang, I creep around the edge of the house and approach my neighbor's boat on the trailer stored in their backyard. I'm proud of myself for thinking of this.

I shiver a little. There's a chill in the air, a typical November day. I ran outside without my sweater. Squatting down next to the boat, I raise the athame against the boat's bottom, scratching the rough stuff from the wood without damaging the hull. Catching what falls into the shoebox, I collect enough for everyone. "Bingo," I say, "Harvesting barnacles this way is ingenious, if I say so." Then I head back inside the house.

My gym bag is wide open, so I put all my collected treasures inside it, along with a black and white candle.

The instructions include a chant or prayer, so I snap a photo of the pages with my phone. A few small black pouches get tossed into the tote, too. Before closing the book, I glimpse a note that says to add turquoise to your bag if you are aiding someone who has lost direction. This certainly applies to our mission. A little bottle of light blue stones from my jewelry-making box gets added before zipping it closed.

I think about Melody a lot, even though she's done some nasty things to me and my friends. Still, I can't help but see her as someone who has lost their way and needs help. She was one of my best buddies. Somewhere deep inside there still is the Melody I know and love. She's just trapped under Blaine Mills' spell.

I lift my bag over one shoulder and fly up the stairs, eager to meet the group and decipher some dreams.

Chapter 12

A CIRCLE OF 7

After slowing down my bike, I lean into a turn onto the gravel pathway of the parking lot for our town lake. Reaching out, I touch the hand-carved wooden sign that reads "Woodland Lake" as I pass by. A smile spreads across my lips as this triggers fond memories of swimming here every summer. It was such an enjoyable time for me.

I hop off the seat and walk the bike the rest of the way in. On the approach to our beloved grassy area on the left, I gaze at the water and grin even more broadly.

What a peaceful setting. I love it. Our group had an unforgettable experience with the energy emanating from our crystals during our ceremony here.

The sound of the crickets chirping in their tiny serenade always offers me tranquility. And the squirrels playing tag with their companions as they dart around in the leaves make me feel one with nature. It's mid-November and the animals are taking advantage of this unusually warm fall day.

"I love this place," I say aloud as I lean my bike against the tree. Hoisting the strap of my gym bag over my head, I take it to the spot where we met the last time. I reach around in my pocket and retrieve a handful of peanuts that I brought for the squirrels, then toss them into the area in which they are playing.

"Oh." I raise my hand to my chest. "You startled me. I assumed I was the first one here."

Sofie reaches out for a hug, then I sit on the log opposite her. "Nice to see you." I don't get to see Sofie every day like the rest of our group because Sofie has already graduated. Although she's not much older than me, she works at the Psychic Connection as an instructor there. She's a shaman and teaches several classes, too. That's where we all met her about a year ago. I take a moment to explain to Sofie the surprise I have planned for today.

We look for the source of laughter before we see the boys. Billy and Jimmy are joking with each other as they hike in.

"Hi, guys." I wave at the two as they near the clearing.

"Hey, Rach," Billy calls out, wrapping his arms around my waist and planting a sweet kiss on my lips. Jimmy waves as he circles us and takes a seat next to Sofie. We join them on the opposite log.

The trees shape a curved canopy over the gravel walkway, as they continue shedding their leaves, and still offer enough shade for anyone on the path. The birds are chatting up a storm as the remaining circle of friends hurries toward us. Clarissa, Jasmine, and Deanna rush and join us on the logs. Each raises their hands in a hello greeting.

A warm, comforting sensation surrounds us all. This happens each time we meet up. It's the energy we bring as it combines with our other pals' vibrations. Almost like pieces of a puzzle coming together for the perfect fit.

"I brought some water for all of us." Deanna rises and distributes the Poland Spring® bottles from her soft-sided cooler bag.

"Thanks, Deanna. What a great idea," Sofie tells her as she pats her back, then sits down next to her. I open my bottle and take a long swig. It's such a hot day. Everyone else follows suit.

Then I speak up. "So, Billy mentioned to me you're having some intense dreams, Jimmy. Can you tell us about them?" I pull no punches. Jimmy smiles and lowers his head, staring at his feet. "It's okay, Jimmy. We're all friends here. There is no judgment. Please, share all the details. Your dream may have some signs to guide us with our Melody situation."

Billy puts his hand on Jimmy's arm in reassurance. "Please tell them what you told me. I know it will help us."

"Let's start the circle first and position our stones, so we all are protected. I believe it will help in making us comfortable, too." Sofie stands and looks around the circle. She is a creature of habit and likes to start her meetings in a certain way. She produces a white candle from her small green satchel and places it on the large flat stone sitting between the two logs, then lights it. Next, she takes her athame blade and runs it through the candle's flame. "The flame represents fire, and the knife through the flame represents air." She holds up the blade and draws a circle in the air. I always love to watch Sofie in action, especially when she's casting a circle. We all watch as she performs her ritual.

"We surround our circle with the salt from the Earth," Sofie says as she takes the container of salt that she brought, opens the spout, and lets it flow as she draws a circle on the surrounding ground. Then she closes the circle once she steps inside by overlapping the lines.

"I like this part," Jasmine whispers.

Sofie grabs her water bottle near her seat, uncaps it, and holds it out. "This is for the element of water." She puts her thumb across the opening and shakes it, spritzing the water around the perimeter as she walks it. Then she raises both arms and speaks, "We have cast the circle using the elements and I have circled 3 times. Now our circle is cast. God, Goddess, and Spirit Guides—please watch over us and protect us".

"Thanks, Sofie. The air is so calming inside our circle. I love it," Jasmine mentions.

Sofie puts her palms together, almost like in prayer, and closes her eyes. Then she bows to Jasmine. As she spreads her arms out wide, she says, "I like to manipulate energy and clear it to share with my friends. I'm glad you guys can sense the effects."

Billy stands up and nods at Sofie. Then he turns to the boy next to him. "Okay, Jimmy–the floor is all yours now. Tell us about your dreams."

Jimmy wipes his palms on his pant legs. "Thanks. I feel calmer now. Whatever Sofie did, it worked. She has the magic touch." He dries his hands again. "I've been having multiple lucid dreams ever since we did the Past Life Ceremony, and they seem so real. I had to say something to Billy."

"Tell us about what you're experiencing. Are all the dreams the same?" Sofie asks him.

"Well. They start the same, but each night I see more of the tale. Like the story is dying to be told. I envision my childhood, but not my current one. In the dream, I am wearing fringed buckskin pants and moccasins, with a feathered headband in my hair. I am young, about 10 years old. I see myself playing with a little girl in a deerskin fringed dress and beaded moccasins. She has ebony hair, woven into long braids. By the third time I dreamt about it, I knew I was staring at a young Melody. So cute. Even though there was no black eyeliner, I was sure it was Mel. We were best friends and soul mates, and we promised we would love and protect each other for eternity. We sealed a special pact."

"You mean our Melody?" I ask, knowing it was her.

"Yes." Jimmy nods his head. "Could be why I'm so drawn to Melody. We promised our love to each other forever."

"Is there more to the story?" Deanna wants to know.

Jimmy makes a weird face. "I wish there was. That is all I've dreamt about so far. The next time, there may be more."

Sofie hands Jimmy a notebook.

"What's this for?" he asks, staring at her.

"It's for you to keep a dream journal. Write everything you can remember about the dream when you wake up." I think we will have the rest of the story within a week.

"Okay, thanks," Jimmy says as he tucks the notebook into his pack behind him.

"That's how we'll get some Intel on how to handle Melody," Billy adds.

"Yes," I agree. The others murmur 'yes' all around.

"Thanks for sharing, Jimmy. You are an important part of this group," Sofie says as she squeezes his shoulder.

"Now, before we leave, Rachel told me she has a surprise for us. Go ahead, Rach." She points to me, palm up.

"Oh, yes," I jump up and grab my bag. "I found this amazing recipe in my mom's new book called *Magic's in the Bag*. And I wanted to try it."

Billy looks up at me. "A recipe for what? Are we making something edible?"

"Well, the book contains recipes for Gris-Gris Bags and Sachets." Now I'm getting confused stares from my friends.

"What the hell is a Gris-Gris Bag?" Billy says what everyone else is probably thinking.

"Kind of like a mojo bag containing herbs and stones for different purposes," I explain. The confused look melts off their faces. I think they get it now.

"Okay, I'll buy that, but what's our purpose?" Billy continues his inquiry. Now he is standing in front of me. All eyes are on me.

I take a deep inhale and confront him. "Just hear me out. You're gonna like this one. The purpose is to protect us from those who wish us harm. Supposedly, it restores balance and if we include some turquoise, it will be of help when aiding someone who has gone off track, like Mel." I return to my seat.

Clarissa stands this time and puts her arms out to her sides. "Are you kidding me? You want to help that bitch who tried to paralyze you?" she shouts.

"Now girls," Sofie positions herself in between us. "Come on, sit." She stares at me with a wary eye.

"Listen, you guys know that Melody and I were the best of friends. I honestly think this Blaine guy is bad news. Things may go back to normal if we can get her away from him. These bags are called 'Good Riddance' bags and they banish negativity and poison from your life. So, if my theory isn't true, then it will help banish Mel too."

There are several moments of silence. Not a pin drops. I tilt my head up and notice the sky is being consumed by clouds and darkness. The wind sweeps my hair into my face.

Billy breaks the stillness. "Okay, I'm in. I say let's do it."

"Me too," Jimmy adds.

"Okay," Clarissa, Jasmine, and Deanna add with hesitation.

"Yes," adds Sofie, as she nods.

Phew. A weight lifts off my shoulders. Walking inside the circle, I continue my mission. I hand each member an empty, tiny black drawstring bag. "Hold these open as I come to you." I show them my baggie of herbs and shake it. "This mixture contains 5 plants." I take a pinch of the mixture and place it in each bag, speaking as I walk around. "Black pepper, Cayenne, lotus flower, and Rue. Don't touch your face after touching this because it will burn." I wipe my hands on my pants.

Jasmine peeks inside the bag. I am sure she can't see anything against the black fabric.

I open two other pouches. "This is sulfur and salt." I sprinkle two pinches in each pouch. Again, I brush the residue from my hands. "You will not believe the last ingredient—barnacles!"

"Where on earth did you get barnacles?" Deanna asks.

"Well, I scraped them from the bottom of my neighbor's boat," I admit.

"Ingenious," Clarissa calls out.

I open the barnacle bag and let each circle member select a barnacle to add to their bag. Then, I hand a black and a white candle to Sofie and ask her to ignite them. She places them on the stone table alongside her candle and lights them with the flame from the pillar. I slip a piece of turquoise into each bag as the last ingredient.

"Please tie your bag closed with three knots and repeat after me..." I tie the knots in mine to show them. "Protect me from those who wish me harm and encircle this bag in a protective white light." The group repeats it. "Cast away evil with this charm to restore balance—absence makes all things right. And help aid our friend who is lost," I add. Only three of the members repeat the last line.

"So mote it be."

We can only hope it banishes the negativity and poison from our lives.

We'll see.

Chapter 13

IT STARTED WITH A WHISPER

That blaring honk is my cue. I grab my tote bag off the chair and practically fly down the steps to the front door.

"Hey Mom, that's Billy. We're going to the library and maybe out for hot chocolate."

Mom peeks out from the kitchen archway with a dishtowel in her hands. She's still in her hospital scrubs, with her hair pulled back into a messy ponytail after a long shift. "Okay, honey. Say hi to Billy for me and be home around 10. It's a school night."

"All right. Catch you later." I swing open the screen door and tap it shut behind me.

I'm glad that I have such a great relationship with my mother. Most of my friends do not. Mom is so easygoing and caring. And she trusts me 100%. I've never given her a reason not to.

Turning toward the blue Mustang parked at the curb, I glance at Billy in the driver's seat, smiling at me and waving like he hasn't seen me in forever. *What a goof!*

As soon as I hop into the car, he leans over and kisses me softly. Then he shifts it in drive and we head off in the library's direction. Minutes later, we glide into the parking lot alongside the building. Billy shuts off the engine and faces me. "You got it, right?"

"Yes, of course." I reach into my pouch. "Right here." I show him you-know-who's spell book. It's the one from her old locker that I unscrupulously gained. I plan to copy it from front to back, including the secret note tucked in the pocket–just for safekeeping. Also, for evidence, should we ever need it. For a moment, guilt gnaws at me.

"Okay, let's go, Nancy Drew." Billy slams his car door and hurries over to my side like a gentleman. Swinging my side open, he offers his hand to help me out. My appreciative smile sets off his as I marvel at his chivalry. "Careful, it's a little slippery."

It's the end of January and I think we just got our first bit of snow, even though it is only a little dusting.

"Thank you." I snatch my bag off the floor and we make our way inside.

We decide to use the copier by the far wall of the building, away from prying eyes. Looking over my shoulder, I make sure the coast is clear. I stealthily remove the book and slide it face-down on the glass. Then I retrieve the handful of coins that I got when I raided my change jar at home and dump them in the plastic trough on the side of the machine. Copies cost ten cents each, so I brought as many dimes as I could find. This hardcover contains twenty-five pages, including the front and back cover, and the hidden, folded yearbook page we discovered by accident.

I complete the task at lightning speed, fold the papers in half, and slip them into my bag with the original. "Mission accomplished."

Billy grins at me. "Okay, my super sleuth." Then he wraps his arm around my waist and presses his lips to mine. I love all the tiny kisses he's been showering me with lately. His mouth grazes my earlobe as he whispers, "Why don't we go back to my house? We can be alone since Mom is not coming home for a while." He winks.

We head over to Billy's place, and I turn to him with a sly little grin. "Nice". I am sure my cheeks are bright pink.

* * *

Billy flips up the mailbox lid and rescues the mail overflowing from the box. "Here, lend me a hand." He hands me a huge handful of envelopes. After turning the key in the lock, the door swings open and hits the wall inside. He says, "You can put it in there," as he points to the basket on the credenza. He slides the deadbolt shut. "The place is all ours now."

I drop the mail.

Then, I coil my arms around my boyfriend's neck and cover his lips with mine. A slow, sensual kiss is exactly what I've been dying to instigate. I press my body tight against him and he pushes me back against the locked door—just like you see in the movies. Passionately, he kisses me in return as his hands roam over my shirt. What a response! I close my eyes, nestle in his arms, and concentrate on his increasing heartbeat, savoring the feel of his warm body.

We stay this way, lip-locked in a heated kissing session, when his thumb inadvertently brushes across my chest, teasing me through the fabric between us. He pulls back to look at me. "Let's move this to my room," he whispers.

I just nod, completely under his spell, as I breathe in the smell of his Axe® body spray.

Billy links his fingers in mine and leads me down the hall to his bedroom at the end. He guides me into his room and kicks the door shut behind us.

Willing my breath to calm down, I stand there for a moment, staring at the geometric pattern on the rug. Billy senses what I am doing and reaches up to run his hand through my hair which helps me relax.

Deep cleansing breaths, he says telepathically. We are in sync with each other. He sits down on the mattress and pats the space beside him. I slide in. Billy strokes my hand and arm, calming my nerves in his wake. He always knows the right thing to do. His hands, now encircling my waist, melt my insides.

Billy's lips search out my lips and we kiss like tomorrow may never come. He leans me down to rest softly on the pillow. The comforter cushions me. My thoughts swirl as his tongue circles mine with caressing strokes. I circle back in response. Billy moves his body, half on top of me, half beside me as his hands roam up and down my body, stopping at the hem of my top. "Can I?" he asks.

"Yes," I softly whisper, as he lifts my shirt over my head and tosses it on his chair.

"Now your turn." I shyly look down as I tug on his tee. He helps me and his top comes off in one swift movement to join mine over where he tossed it. He leans against me. Skin-to-skin.

Wrapping my arm around his neck, I pull him closer. We smooch again and again. Returning his deepening kiss with intensity, my body tingles with electricity while my heart pounds out of control. I reach up with my fingers, sliding them through his chest hair as I lean forward to kiss his pecks. So tight. His body against mine takes my breath away.

Billy stretches up as he caresses my cheek with his thumb, moving tiny kisses from my lips down along my collarbone, taking little nibbles along the route as he dives down to my cleavage.

Lightning shoots right through me.

I gasp.

My head is spinning.

Sliding my hands on both of his cheeks, I lead his mouth back up to mine. My breath comes out in short, panting spurts. My entire body trembles and is on the verge of something I don't quite understand.

A low growl escapes his lips as I brace for his next move. Billy and I have been going out for a while, so I know things would escalate, eventually. He teases me by tracing little circles with his fingertips against my exposed skin. I draw in a quick breath. The feel of his skin against mine is nothing as I'd ever imagined.

I shiver.

"Is it too much?" he asks softly, his breathing erratic. I can feel his body rigid against my hip.

"No," I barely manage as I lift his chin for another kiss.

He smooths down my hair as he whispers, "Tell me to stop and I will." Reaching over to me, he unbuttons my pants and helps me wiggle out of them. Then he quickly stands and drops his jeans to the floor.

My eyes go wide.

"You sure your mom won't walk in on us?"

"Nope, she isn't coming home until after 9 tonight. The place is all ours." Billy pulls me to my feet and wraps me in a bear hug. His body pushes tight against me.

I melt.

"God, you're beautiful," he tells me before his lips crush into mine.

"Thanks," I murmur. *How do you respond to that?* "You're not so bad yourself." My voice shakes.

"You're cold," he says as he grabs the covers and pushes them down on the bed. "Let's get under the sheets."

So, I slide in between the plaid sheets, hoping he doesn't notice my sweaty palms. I pull him in next to me and he tugs up the top sheet halfway. He guides my hand between our bodies, but I'm not sure what to do, so I explore a bit. *Oh, my!*

Why thank you! I hear telepathically. I am glad the lights are out because I know I am blushing. Big time.

He puts his hand on mine for some guidance and after several minutes; he steadies them. "That's enough for now. You'll undo me."

I take in a deep breath and expel it slowly. I'm relieved. By the light of his alarm clock on his nightstand, I can see Billy with that lopsided grin I love so much. He leans forward and gently kisses my lips and my neck. My heart hammers.

Focus, focus, I tell myself, so I don't panic.

He stops at my ear and whispers, "I would never do anything to hurt you."

I nod. *I know that.*

When Billy eases me onto my back, he does some crazy, insane things with his hand that floods me with a rush of sensations. I take in a sharp breath as tiny electrical impulses dance in response to his touch. It gets to a point of no return and I collapse into his arms. He holds me tight for a few minutes, then looks up at me lovingly and gives me a passionate kiss, running his hands along my arms to calm me once again. He pauses for a moment.

"Rachel, I think I love you." It comes out in a husky voice.

Not expecting this at all, it takes me a while to respond. "I... um... love you, too." *Oh, no, I know where this is going and I am not ready for that next step.*

"Just breathe." Billy strokes my cheek. *Me neither*, he tells me telepathically. I'm finding it hard to look him in the face after his confession.

He wraps me in a cocoon and cradles my head. "That's my girl." His heart beats wildly against me. Then he takes my hand. "You feel so amazing."

Billy guides me as we gently continue to explore each other. His heartbeat ramps from wild to savage, pounding against his ribs as he holds his breath for a brief second or two, then crushes my lips with his kiss. It is so beautiful, so intoxicating, so forbidden. We hold our embrace for a long while until our heart rhythms return to a normal pace and our breathing slows naturally. He kisses me again and we get lost in each other for a second time.

As he rakes his hand through his messy locks, I think to myself–*he is so handsome*. I glance down at the tousled sheets, our clothes strewn on the chair, and the crumbled tissues on the floor. *We need to clean up this mess!*

I know, Billy mentally responds with a laugh as he retrieves my shirt from the pile and tosses it to me, backhanded. We quickly get dressed and attempt to straighten up the room before his mother comes home.

We just forged a closer emotional bond between us. Billy is all I ever want, so loving, so gentle, so understanding. And he's all mine!

Chapter 14

BAD NEWS

The house lights in the auditorium gradually come up. Most of the student body is blinking their eyes to adjust from darkness to light. And my friends and I applaud at the last curtain call of the school play, 'Bye, Bye, Birdie.' The drama club gave an exceptional performance this year. I'll be humming the tunes in my head for the next few weeks.

Crackling from the microphone draws our attention to Principal Keane taking center stage, asking us to settle down and take our seats for a very important announcement. Once we all sit, the microphone comes alive again.

"Boys and Girls, I want to use this opportunity to tell you about some updates on the Midsummer Night's Dream Costume Ball. Unfortunately, we don't have enough tickets sold, so we had to choose to either cancel it or share it with another school. And we did just that. We will share the ball with Toledo High in the next town."

The noise level in the auditorium raises an octave with the audience's disapproval.

"Now, wait a minute… settle down." The principal tries to gain control. "This is the most efficient way to save the event. I've discussed it with their principal and Toledo is very excited to join us. Our students will be on one side of the ballroom, and theirs will sit on the opposite side. We'll share in the food, photo-taking, dancing, and the band. Since we cannot sell enough tickets to cover the costs of the ball, we made the arrangements."

Vice Principal Rizzo takes the microphone and tells us all to go to our next class.

I hang my head in my hands. Toledo is the town that Melody moved to. Mel and her shady boyfriend could show up at our Ball. This is going to be disastrous.

Billy bends down to hug me. He doesn't even have to speak. I can hear his thoughts in my mind. *Shit. This is gonna suck.*

My sentiments exactly, I reply. I lift my head and glance at my circle of friends. They all know the situation. No words are necessary. We will need to prepare ourselves for a close encounter with the enemy.

Just great!

* * *

A few of us make our way to Curley's Ice Cream after school. We are sitting in the back of the building at an indoor picnic table area for patrons. I'm digging into my Vanilla Dusty Road Ice Cream Sundae and licking my lips. It tastes so darn good. With me are Billy, Jimmy, Jasmine, and Deanna. They wanted to meet to discuss some questions they had regarding Melody and Blaine and how we met. They're just looking for some answers. First things first though, we work on our desserts. Billy is a chocolate guy through and through. He slurps up his Chocolate Milkshake with a large straw. Jimmy and he both ordered the same thing. Jasmine and Deanna are sharing a jumbo Banana Split. So, we spend about ten minutes enjoying the nice weather and luscious desserts.

After we made a dent in our ice cream, Jimmy brings up his questions. "I'd like to know how you met Blaine in the first place. And why is he the bad guy? What happened?

"Well, it's a tangled story, for sure," I say. "Initially I met him under a different name. His name was Brandon, and I met him with his two buddies– Josh and Drew- at the Witches' Ball last Halloween at the Psychic Connection. Brandon tagged along with his sister who often came to events at the store. I was at the party with Clarissa and Melody."

"That's right. I remember it now. You and Clarissa told me all about it. She said you guys were having fun until you got separated. Mel and Drew went to get some punch. Then Clarissa warned you to be careful before she and Josh went to get some food. That left you alone with Brandon," Jasmine added.

"Wait a minute," Jimmy cuts in. I don't understand. Why was his name Brandon first, but now it's Blaine?"

I shrug my shoulders. "All I know is that his real name was Brandon. He was just a regular-looking guy with brown spikey hair, not the goth-looking kid he is now. I think he may have changed his name when he joined the coven that Mel belonged to."

"Okay." Jimmy seemed satisfied with that.

Then I continued, "So at the party, I started to feel a bit light-headed with ringing in my ears. I think someone spiked the punch. Brandon's dreamy brown eyes and sultry smile made me fall for him. I followed him to take a walk in the woods. We came upon a clearing with several huge stone seats."

Billy seemed fidgety listening to the story again. "Can you make this long story a bit shorter?

"Okay, okay." I reach over and place my hand on his for reassurance. "Back to the story- so Brandon sat down with me and in a matter of seconds, he went in for the kiss. He kissed me hard and fast. I liked it. The next thing I knew the kid was all hands, molesting me, touching me in places I didn't want to be touched. I pushed him away so hard I hurt him, but it didn't stop him. I was alone with a drunken maniac. This is important to remember – with his arms wrapped around me so tight he was slurring his words, 'Come on, you want it, you know you like it.' And he kissed my lips and my neck." I shudder at that memory.

"So, how did you get away?" Deanna asked.

"Well, the whole time I was calling to Billy over and over in my head. Praying he would hear me. He did and came tearing down the path, leaped onto Brandon using his wrestling moves around Brandon's neck. I thought he was going to kill him."

Billy takes over. "I remember this very clearly. I yelled at him, 'If you ever touch her again, I will kill you. Hands off!' Then Rachel convinced me to let him go."

I look over at Billy next to me on the picnic bench. His face is all red like he's re-living that moment. "Billy, you saved me!" I squeeze his arm.

"Now I see why you don't like him," Deanna says.

I shake my head and walk over to toss out my trash. "So, the second part of the story is when Jasmine and I both met Mel's new boyfriend." I glance over toward Jasmine.

"Rachel and I went to the Beltane Festival on May 1st. We were meeting Mel, and she brought her new guy," Jasmine adds.

I continue, "We both sat at a picnic table and Mel introduced us to her new friend, Blaine, who belonged to the same coven she did. He looked just like her with black eyeliner, jewelry, and black nail polish. Something was familiar about his eyes and it chilled me to the bone. It spooked me. After the meeting, we all participated in the Maypole dance, weaving in and out of the long ribbons, and dancing to the music. It kind of took the edge off. In the end, we hugged the person to our right, then the one to our left. To my left was Blaine, and he hugged me a little too long. When I tried to break away, he whispered, 'You know you like it.' My body went stiff and my inner self was shouting—*Get Away from Him!*"

"Oh, My God, Rachel," Jimmy says. "Now, I understand why he's the bad guy. He's pure evil."

"And that is how we met."

Chapter 15

HAND-IN-HAND

Mother Nature can't make up her mind today. The sky shows grayish with white clouds skittering through at a quick pace. It darkens its tone and covers the sun, but just for a few minutes, then the scene flips back to gray. In like a lion and out like a lamb.

I glance around the room that I am in, admiring the red and black decorations adorning the den. Jasmine's mother collects these oriental paintings that depict lotus blossoms surrounding ornate Chinese lettering. She tells us they represent love, life, and happiness. Today, we are holding another Psychic Circle meeting in her den.

"Hi, Jazz," I say as I place the stones that I brought onto the low, shiny black table in the center of the room. She smiles and nods as she continues to arrange her other trinkets around them. The signature scent of Nag Champa incense infuses the air. "Your mom let me in."

"Okay."

Right on time. The others are descending the stairs behind me. Billy, Sofie, Clarissa, Deanna, and Jimmy. We all settle in by getting comfortable on the low, red velvet sofas and two black padded chairs in the room.

Sofie stands. "Glad you all could make it. We need to have our sessions more often, so we get more practice using our psychic abilities. I know Rachel's been having some repetitive dreams lately. Can you tell us about them?" She directs the question at me. Then she sits back down.

I clear my throat and nervously rub my necklace before I begin. "Well, I thought we'd try something I've been dreaming about. Call it strange, but I've had this recurring dream three times this week."

"Okay, let us know more and we'll give it a go," Sofie says.

I stand up and smooth my pants, keeping my feet about a foot apart. "Please humor me and do as I do. I'd rather show than tell."

Everyone in the circle stands a little closer and mimics my stance.

"So, I've been dreaming of our circle meeting, and we are all standing like this together. We link hands one by one in a ceremonial manner. Just watch."

I twist toward Billy, link my left hand to his right, then look into his eyes as I say, "Hand-in-hand, we cast this circle. Next, you turn to Sofie and do the same."

Billy turns left toward Sofie. He reaches for her hand and clasps it, saying, "Hand-in-hand, we cast this circle."

I interject, "Look at her eyes when you say it. I know it sounds corny, but let's try to do it exactly like in my dream."

He repeats his motions to my specifications, obviously trying not to laugh.

Sofie turns toward Jasmine, smiling as their eyes meet and she continues the mantra, "Hand-in-hand, we cast this circle," while grasping her outstretched hand.

It's almost as if we opened up a channel of energy as it suddenly flows through our linked hands. The static charge is undeniable.

I can't help but smile. "Keep it going–do you feel that?"

The group nods together as one. We continue around the circle as Sofie turns to Clarissa, links hands, and says the seven magic words.

"This is awesome," Clarissa whispers.

Next to Clarissa is Deanna, who continues to link hands and speaks the mantra. And last, Deanna links up with Jimmy. He is visibly trembling as the energy flows through him. He reaches for my hand and meets my eyes. A single tear glistens in the inner corner of his eye as he utters the magic words: "Hand-in-hand, we cast this circle." With that, an electrical zap cements our circle. We stand here for a moment and let the pulse circle the room, slow but steady. It moves from person to person, providing us with a floating feeling.

Sofie speaks up. "Let's make sure we ground ourselves as we continue this exercise. Mentally, send a portion of this energy down through your legs, continuing down through the earth as roots from a tree would grow. We've done this before."

We all instinctually close our eyes and attempt to visualize Sofie's instructions.

I can feel the energy ground us, binding our bodies to the earth. I'm still tingly, but at least the floating has diminished. With that under control, I explain more of my dream. "So, in my dream, we could direct the energy, making it stop and start at will. To start it up again, imagine this energy emanating from your heart. Push it down your left arm to your hand and fingers, and now urge it on through to your neighbor's body. If we each visualize this simultaneously, we will move the energy around our circle at will. Let's try."

With our hands still connected, we practice moving this energy and stopping it, speeding it up and slowing it down. We are on a high!

My hands and arms tingle as the energy brushes the surface. Even my lips are tingly. I know we are all sensing it.

"This is so cool," Jasmine says with a giggle.

"Yes." Deanna squeezes Jimmy's hand to comfort him. I can tell she senses he is being overwhelmed.

Here we are sharing this collective energy, pushing it from one person to the other and receiving it from them. I secretly want to see if we can share the secret thing we did in my dream, telling none of them about it beforehand.

I close my eyes and build up the energy in my body. Using all my might, I push out a silent message through the circle. It should reach each one of them –

Say "yes" out loud if you can hear it in your mind.

I sit in silence for a brief second and I hear it first from Billy– "Yes."

Then Sofie– "Yes".

Jasmine– "Yes".

Clarissa– "Yes".

Deanna– "Yes".

All eyes are on Jimmy. "What?" he says as he looks up at me. A smile erupts on his face. "Yes, yes."

"That is exactly what I dreamt about. Don't break the circle yet. We have to do something with all this energy. First, let's send the energy fast around our circle, revving it up. Then, count to 3 and break hands, then we can send out our energy to help heal this awful pandemic."

I open my eyes to peek at our group. The concentration on each of their faces shows it all.

"Here we go–faster and faster. Now, 1-2-3–let go and raise your hands high. Send this energy as a cure."

All the members stand up together and we stretch to the heavens for what seems like five minutes. I was the first to collapse back in my seat, followed by Sofie. The others follow soon after us. We lounge here in silence for several moments to regroup. The only sound is the heavy breathing of our circle, trying to calm their bodies down.

It's a delightful feeling when your dreams come true.

Very satisfying.

Chapter 16

DREAMS WON'T STOP

I'm wickedly proud of the work we did and how we connected our energies so fast. It blows my mind that we could control the flow of that energy and send it off to help heal the world during the Pandemic.

I look up while exiting Jasmine's house, noticing that the painted gray sky is promising rain. The achiness in my arm is a telltale sign. It hasn't been the same since I broke it two years ago. I automatically rub it and follow Billy to his car as the screen door slams behind us. Looking over my shoulder, I see Jimmy running to catch up.

"Hey guys, wait up," Jimmy calls out as he raises his index finger. "I need to talk with both of you." He catches up to us.

"Hop in, and we can hit the park and chat if you're up for it." Billy motions for him to climb in the back.

"Okay."

I swing open the door of Billy's blue Mustang and push the passenger seat forward to allow room for Jimmy to climb in. Then I adjust the seat again and slide in.

Billy checks his rearview mirror before we take off toward the town park. The sky is cloudy and getting that darker shade of gray already. We may be in for some more rain- April showers bring May flowers. But we pull into the adjacent parking lot anyway, even though the place is closed. A gate and turnstile are here to count the guests as they enter. This way they are aware of how many people are in the park at any time. From the lot, I can see the swimming lake, bathhouse, and picnic area.

Billy turns off the engine and everyone gets out. Jimmy and I follow him as he jumps over the turnstile and ventures toward a picnic table. Jimmy hops over the barricade too and leans back, extending his hand to help me climb over. And we join Billy on the bench.

"What's going on?" Billy cuts to the chase.

Jimmy looks at us. "I was too nervous to mention it at our meeting, but my dreams have been more frequent. I keep having the dream of when Mel and I were young and made that pact between us to love and protect each other for eternity–that we were soulmates. And I could hear Mel's voice so clearly in my dream, 'Remember, for eternity, forever.' I get the chills every time I think of it."

"Did you see her face up close? Are you sure it was her?" I ask.

"There is no doubt in my mind. It was Mel. I could see every freckle on her face, every line on her skin. I'd recognize those eyes anywhere."

Billy stands up and walks toward the edge of the beach area, staring off and contemplating something. Then he comes back to us. "What do you think this means? Was there anything more to the dream?"

"I... I don't know." Jimmy shakes his head. "Well, I just have this strong feeling that I have to help her. My mind is filled with these thoughts, like someone is whispering in my ear. It's all so strange." Jimmy paces back and forth in front of Billy and me. "I've been jotting all these little thoughts in my notebook all week."

"Go ahead, Jimmy, tell us more about what you've been getting. Perhaps we can figure this thing out." I urge him on, trying to be supportive. He seems very nervous about this whole darn experience.

Jimmy reaches back into the pocket of his jeans and retrieves a mini notebook. His hand shakes like a leaf as he opens it. He goes on, "That voice tells me that this guy Blaine knows of the strong connection between Melody and me. He is also aware of our karmic pact. This dude is an incredibly powerful warlock who cast a wicked spell on Mel for her to turn a blind eye to me in order to sabotage our bond."

"What?" I shake my head. I can't believe what I am hearing. "So, Mel is living this life with blinders on?" I wring my hands and grit my teeth. "Blaine is such a manipulative bastard!"

Billy reaches over and puts his hand on my back and rubs it in little circles. He knows I am pissed.

"I think that my spirit guide has also been visiting me too," Jimmy confides as he sits back down. "I've seen him in my sleep. He reminds me of an old wizard, sort of like Hogwarts's headmaster. Last night, he visited me and said that these manipulations have been going on for centuries. Blaine secretly knew we would all reincarnate together in this lifetime. There is a Super Moon and a Total Lunar Eclipse at the same time this year. A double whammy. This is the event that Blaine picked to bring Melody to his dark side."

Billy and I are both listening with surprised looks on our faces.

"We learned about that Super Moon in Science class this week. That's when the earth, the sun, and a full moon line up perfectly, and the moon moves into the Earth's shadow," I tell them.

Billy sits there scratching his head. "I don't get it. What's with Mel's infatuation with me? Was that also set up by that monster?"

"But wait..." I interject. "Melody told me she always wanted what I had. So, she wanted you since I had you." I point to Billy. "I don't know if Blaine is smart enough to put it in place."

Jimmy leans forward on the edge of the bench. "You know what... if this guy is such a powerful warlock, then maybe he came up with a sinister plan to have Mel become obsessed with Billy. This would make Rachel jealous of it all. That would break Rachel's tight bond with Mel, which would leave Melody wide open for his energy grab. He wants her power, right?"

"Now that's messed up!" Billy shakes his head; his cheeks are a burning shade of crimson.

I ponder that scenario for a moment and blurt out, "My God, Jimmy, I think you hit the nail on the head. You're a super sleuth–you've uncovered his evil plan. Oh, what a tangled web we weave..."

"You said it," Billy adds as he steps over to Jimmy and raises his hand in a high five, then uses his other hand to slap my back.

The three of us grab a group hug and walk over to the car. Billy tells us along the way, "Melody and Rachel had such a strong bond that could've ruined all of Blaine's plans. We can't let that happen because he has been trying to split them up since forever.

Not on my watch!

Chapter 17

UNDER A BLOOD-RED MOON

Saturday, April 29th – It's nice to end the month with a calming sky for once. The sun is still dancing near the horizon and the outline of the moon is beginning to make its appearance in the sky. I can't believe that in a couple of days, it will be May already.

Sofie called for an emergency meeting of the Psychic Circle, considering all that has gone on lately. It seems like we have been getting together almost every other day.

It's crystal time!

Today's location is in my basement. Sofie has a special request this time. She had me ask each member to bring their special crystals, so we can work on "programming" our crystals.

Right now, I'm rearranging the furniture and adding some folding chairs between the couches so that we may have a better view of each other. After shaking out a purple and black cloth covered in runic symbols, I flip it, so it lays over the old sea trunk in the middle of the room. A huge, raw amethyst stone I place in the center to provide us extra loving, calming energy while we work. My new abalone shell containing some sage is the last thing I add to the top of the chest. This should offer us additional protection during our session.

The first to arrive is Billy. My mom let him in the front door, and now he's bounding down the basement steps, taking two at a time, the way he usually does. That's what gives him away all the time. He stops inches from me and flashes that million-dollar smile before he plants a gentle kiss on my waiting lips. "Mmm…" Billy softly groans as I feel the ticklish vibration around my mouth. I wrap my arms around his neck and pull him closer. He tucks his hands in the back pockets of my jeans.

Suddenly, I sense movement beside us as Jimmy comes bolting down the steps and pushes past. "Get a room," he says in passing.

We break our embrace and giggle like kids.

"Hi," I greet him.

I hear the screen door open and close several times, and the girls approach us, one right after the other. First, I notice Jasmine's beautiful red satin chemise top and her gold necklace with a shiny golden Chinese symbol dangling from the chain. She sees me admiring it and says, "It's for good luck."

"I love it," I reply as I hug her.

"Brought some chips to munch on." She holds up the chip bag.

"Yay."

Behind her is Clarissa, who smiles at me as I give a high-five. She hands me a 2-liter bottle of Cola that I add to the table near the couches.

Sofie and Deanna bring up the rear, bearing chocolate chip cookies and pretzels. I proceed with my hugs, then put the food down as everyone gets comfy. The boys have already taken their seats on the far sofa.

"Love your trunk table," Sofie comments as she runs her hand along the runic signs decorating the table scarf.

"That's the trunk that Mom and I refinished a while ago." Then I turn to the group. "Thanks for coming, everyone. Please put your stones on the trunk directly in front of you. We will focus on these today. It's important to prime them in time for the 'Midsummer Night's Dream Ball.'" I take out my two clear quartz crystals and place them in front of me.

Billy stands up and pulls the shiny black hematite stone from his pocket and places it next to mine. Jasmine also brought her hematite and lays it down on the cloth. Then she moves her hands in a praying position and does a quick bow, a typical Jasmine motion. Clarissa and Sofie add their agates to the mix.

"Here's mine." Deanna leans over and adds a rose quartz stone in the shape of a heart, being careful not to let the fringe of her crochet vest touch the candles. "Rose quartz is a very loving stone."

"I always carry a smooth amethyst in my pocket. It carries healing ability." Jimmy bends over and adds it to the gemstone mix.

"Hey Sofie, can you tell us what's so special about tonight?" I turn in her direction.

"Yes, tonight is that Super Moon event you guys learned about in your science class. This is an extremely powerful night, and we should use it to our advantage."

I add, "So basically, we're going to use the moon and the sun's combined energy to recharge our crystals again. In school, we learned the moon takes on a ruddy red hue during a total lunar eclipse of a full moon. The blood-red moon gets its hue from the scattering of sunlight through the earth's atmosphere."

Jasmine leans forward and says, "So by celebrating both the light and the dark, along with the masculine and the feminine energy of this event, we can also empower the truth of the world to pervade in the stones."

"Absolutely, I like that," Sofie responds.

"Me too," Deanna agrees. The others nod.

"Since this is all about the moon in the sky, Rachel, can you open the Bilco cellar doors so we can see the moon and its red glow tonight?" Sofie asks.

"Sure thing." I rise and unlock the slanted doors that lead to the backyard and push them open. It gives us a perfect view of the night sky. The shadow almost covers the moon, and a blood-red hue is appearing. Everyone gets up and crowds around me, peering out into the night.

The power in the room is escalating, resulting in little electrical shocks I can detect on my arms.

"Wow!" Jimmy admires the scene. He feels the pulses, too.

"Okay, let's all sit back down and start, so we don't miss this chance." Sofie corrals the group back to the circle. "We can still see the moon from here."

"Should we take our shoes off to ground our feet?" Clarissa directs her question at Sofie.

"Good idea. Take them off." We all remove our shoes and push them to the side.

I light the four white candles on the table and turn off the overhead light as Sofie takes a container of salt and draws a continuous salt line in a circle around the couches and all of us. "We're going to clean that up when we are done, so your mom doesn't have a fit," Sofie mentions to me and I answer with a giggle.

"Let's cast our circle. Please, hold your crystal while you visualize an enormous bubble surrounding the room. It will keep us safe and maximize our intentions," Sofie says. "This is a good mantra I heard on the Salem Live Ghost Hunt that was on the Discovery Channel. Repeat each line after me–

Earth is my body.
Air is my breath.
Fire is my spirit.
Water is my blood.
I cast this protective circle
In perfect love and perfect trust.
So mote it be.

Stay inside this circle until we are done."

We all turn our heads toward the cellar door area. The moon is now almost covered, and the sun's last rays are shining through. We're bathed in the light of the blood-red moon.

"Please display your stones about waist high, flat on your palms." Sofie holds hers out to show us. Then she calls out, "Energy of the sun—we call to you, Energy of the moon—we call to you. Aid us in our quest. Energize our stones. Help us in our call for protection and dispel our fears."

We each glance around the room to view our circle of friends in action and turn to stare at the moon.

"Now raise your palms to eye level and focus on your stones. The crystals are going to energize us and help heal the mind and spirit. They will alter our fears. Hematite stones are going to protect us by repelling negativity. Agates act as security, grounding, and protection. Amethyst helps in healing. And the Rose Quartz will add much-needed love." Sofie instructs. At that moment, the crystals and gemstones tickle my hand as they vibrate slightly, absorbing their programming with the help of the sun and moon.

"Holy shit, the stones are moving!" Billy calls out.

"Mine too," Jimmy adds.

"Uh, huh," the rest of us say in agreement.

I suck in a quick breath. "Look at that... can you believe it? I can see the tiny streams of moonlight and sunlight enter the room and seek out the stones. "Are you guys seeing this?" I ask aloud.

"Yes, awesome!" I hear all around.

An extraordinary warmth penetrates my stones as they absorb the light. "It's so warm. I can't believe this is happening," I tell them.

"Me neither," Jasmine agrees. We remain here for a few moments, basking in what moonlight remains.

"Ok, I'm going to call it before this situation gets too intense." Sofie lowers her palms and lets her stones tumble from them back onto the table. Then she stands up to help the others. We sit still for a few more minutes, shaking our hands to cool them off.

"That was incredible!" Billy says, loudly.

"Don't leave yet. Let's show gratitude-We give thanks to the elements for protecting our circle and thank you to the moon and the sun for energizing our crystals with their combined super-energy this night. Amen." Sofie puts her palms together and bows.

"Amen."

"Please bring your stones to the Midsummer Night's Dream Ball in your pocket or your purse. We may need their help, especially if a certain someone and her evil boyfriend decide to show up." I fold my hands, palm to palm, as if praying and bow to the group.

One can never be too careful.

Chapter 18

A MIDSUMMER NIGHT'S DREAM

It's the first Saturday in May. Our Midsummer Night's Dream Costume Ball has finally arrived. We've been planning and preparing for this event for weeks, and it has now come to fruition. With dreamy eyes like Cinderella, I glance up at my costume hanging from my closet door. As I scan the beautiful satin gown, I am compelled to touch the silky, black, strapless bodice. I can't believe it's mine. The fabric is so smooth. The metal hardware accents across the back and front and the leather accent straps encircling the upper arms sold me. When I'm in it, I am a glorious warrior. It's so badass. This is what you call steam-punk, for sure. It will be quite a night.

I search through my closet for the small leather drawstring pouch I bought at the Renaissance Fair last year. It hangs from long, thin leather straps that will compliment my dress. It is the perfect size for my cellphone, my crystals, lipstick, and some money. Ah, here it is. I pull it out and toss it on the bed. My black patent-leather ankle boots are the perfect accent. I'm all set.

Deanna and Sofie don't attend our school, so they would have to be a guest of someone from this school district. Jasmine has asked Deanna to be her date to the ball, and Clarissa said Sofie will be her 'plus one'. Billy is my date and Jimmy is going stag.

Together, we have decided we can't afford a limo, especially if we want to go down the shore the next day, so we are taking two cars—Jimmy and I will drive with Billy. Clarissa will have the three others in her car. Problem solved, in case we decide to do the shore thing.

Oh my gosh, Billy is arriving in less than an hour, so I need to speed up. I strip off my clothes and put on the special strapless undergarment for my gown, then unzip the gown so I can wiggle into the voluminous layers. The zipping up part goes smoother than I thought it would with a side zipper. I step over to my full-length mirror and gasp. I look so grown-up like I'm in college.

Hoping that my bag is big enough for all my stuff, I slip the two quartz crystals into the leather pouch along with my school ID, money, ticket, and phone. It fits. After applying my makeup, the lipstick goes in the bag too. Perfect fit. Gathering a few locks near my face, I curl them with the curling wand for touch-ups and apply some hair spray. Then, I secure the clasp of my beautiful labradorite necklace close to my neck. Just a spritz of my new perfume called 'Poison' and I do the model spin through the cloud of scent.

"Hey, Mom...," I call out. "Got a minute?" I hear her bare feet padding down the hallway toward my room. The door flies open, then she hurries in, eager to help.

"Wow, you look amazing, Rachel!" I notice her eyes glistening. "My baby's all grown up." She embraces me in a warm hug, which makes me smile.

"Thanks, Mom. Can you help me with these arm bracelets?"

"Oh, okay, honey. Let me check the package for directions." She studies the instructions. "I get it now." Mom wraps the cord and the metal accents around each arm like an expert. "I think you're all set."

"Just in time. Thanks again, Mom. I think that's Billy. See you tonight."

My mother follows me downstairs and waves to Billy outside. "Have fun, you two! Take pictures and be safe."

Billy gets out and opens the car door for me. "You look gorgeous, babe," he whispers in my ear and gives me a quick kiss. Then he helps me fold my dress around my body to tuck me in the vehicle. Next, we go to pick up Jimmy.

* * *

My pulse picks up its tempo as we pull into the Venetian Village entrance off Route 23. The long driveway leads straight to the main building, which resembles a majestic castle. Several other buildings and alleyways snake off the main circle drive, like a small village. In the center of the circle, an exquisite lighted carousel is already in motion. It's so beautiful. The decorating committee strung fairy lights from the carousel top to the main entrance archway. Billy drops his Mustang off by the valet station after we step out of the vehicle. Then, they usher us through the entrance doors.

I tip my head and steal a side-eyed glance, admiring Billy in his costume. Dressed in a purple vest, a white frilly shirt with gathered cuffs, and dark pants. When I wasn't looking, he must have put on his black mask. I try to hold back my grin when I see it.

"Hold on a minute," I say. I walk over to a mirror on the wall to slip on my black satin mask. Then I turn and curtsy. We both bust out a laugh.

Jimmy has an outfit similar to Billy's costume, except his vest is green with a green satin mask.

Straight down the hall, we spot an enormous sign pointing to the main ballroom, where our party begins. We check in at the desk and show our tickets to get our hands stamped, so we can come and go as we please. The lights draw our eyes up to the ceiling as we enter. Millions of tiny fairy lights hang from the sparkly tulle fabric draped from the center of the room to the corners and sides of the ballroom. It reminds me of a magical fairytale tent.

"Wow, you guys did an exceptional decorating job, Rach," Billy says as he links arms with me to go find our table. They assigned our group to table number 5.

Twenty-four round tables encircle the dance floor in a stunning array. The green and gold tablecloths, accented by moss table runners, show off the centerpieces of white floating candles in tall cylindrical vases. They spread glitter across the center of the table. How magical!

"Here we are," Jimmy says as he locates Table 5, pulls out a chair, and plops himself down. The hosts set place cards with our names on them reserving our seats for the evening.

"Before we get settled in, let's check out the rest of the venue," Billy suggests as he pats Jimmy on the back. The three of us walk to the garden area. At the entrance to the garden stands a white garden gate set up beneath a trellis of roses and fairy lights. Tiny elves and fairies peek out from an artificial tree, off to the left. I can smell the roses; they must be real. A white wooden garden swing hangs from ropes strung over the limbs. There is a sign - Stop for your photo here. No line. Taking advantage of the opportunity, we sit on the swing to have our picture taken. The photographer snaps the shot. Since Jimmy is alone, Billy and I photo-bomb his shot with a high-five above him.

"This is much more than I expected," Jimmy admits. "Great job, Rach."

"Thanks," I reply as I push open the gate. It leads us to the outside garden.

They strung more glittery lights about the ornamental garden, with a three-tiered water fountain in the center of the garden. Each tier's water cascade lights up with a different color -

purple, gold, and green in an illuminating display. The theater department decorated this section with little elves, fairies, and cement gnomes positioned throughout the area amidst the colorful flowers, herbs, and rocks. The path, lined with big ten-inch lanterns, gives it a magical touch.

More guests have arrived. So, we head back to our table, where we find the rest of our gang settling in their seats.

"Hi, guys," I shout, waving my hand and rushing toward them.

The first friend I come to is Jasmine in her golden Grecian-style gown with crisscrossed scarves across the front. "You are gorgeous!" I hug her right away.

"You, too." She checks me over. "Wow!"

Deanna sits beside her in a silky brown and green ruffled wrap dress. Her Aunt Jessie works for a big designer in New York City and scored a sample gown for her. "Fabulous." I say as we hug.

Clarissa looks exquisite in her light green gown with sheer green gypsy layers across it. "Love it, love it!" I try to squeeze in behind the table as I hug her, too.

I reach over to touch Sofie's arm — no room to hug her here. She's wedged into the corner. Her white gauzy gown with ruffles, a very down-to-earth Bohemian-style gown works perfectly for her. We strain to high-five each other.

As we sit down, the servers serve the food. Our dinners are our choice of stuffed chicken breast, salmon, or steak. Each comes with a vegetable, potato, and salad. We pre-selected our meal choice when we signed up.

As we are about to dig in, the microphone comes to life. "Welcome to our Midsummer Night's Dream Costume Ball. We have wonderful things planned for tonight. You can get your photo taken by the garden swing and stroll through the enchanted garden. Be sure to take a ride on the huge carousel on the front lawn. We will be sharing our night with Toledo High. Please welcome them. Enjoy your meal and we will talk again later. Bon appétit!" The principal made his speech short and sweet.

Once all the guests enjoy their meals, the conversation automatically starts back up. I glance around the room to see the guests and their dates. The room lights suddenly dim, which gives it a nice, warm ambiance. "Has anyone seen you-know-who?" I ask my table mates. Each shakes their head back and forth, causing my dry mouth to be more parched than it is. I guzzle down the water in my glass.

After dinner, the DJ plays music for those who want to dance. The dangling overhead lights pulse to the beat. The next thing I know, I'm being tugged onto the dance floor by Clarissa, and the rest of the girls follow us. Billy and Jimmy want nothing to do with dancing, so it's just us girls, dancing in our little circle, having a great time when I spot them.

We see Melody and Blaine seated at a table on the other side of the dance floor. Mel's eyes appear glazed over like she is staring into space. Of course, Blaine wraps his arms around her, and he strokes her arm as he whispers in her ear. Maybe she's drunk or drugged - I don't know. Or maybe he has her under a spell. I watch them rise from their seats and notice he is forcefully pulling her by her arm, leading her outside toward the garden gate.

Up to no good, I'll bet.
Something doesn't sit right with me.

Chapter 19

VILLAGE SHENANIGANS

What's going on, Rach? I hear Billy, right away, he's in my head.

I ignore him.

Quickly, I turn and rush after Blaine and Melody. It's so obvious that he is controlling her; I can see it in her eyes. The garden gate snaps shut in front of me just as I reach it. I push it open in time to glimpse the black fabric of Melody's gown swoosh by as the two of them round the corner a few hundred feet ahead. Selecting one of the shining lanterns along the path, I snatch it as I go by. With my free hand, I pull out a quartz crystal from my pouch. Maneuvering the crystal to align it, I position it in my left hand like I would hold a sword and adjust my grip on the ten-inch lantern in my right.

I am going to find them, I vow to myself.

Find who? I hear Billy's thoughts.

Ask my friends, I respond abruptly.

I venture out of the second gate, located toward the back of the garden, which takes me out to the village alleyways. There is no sight of them. The sky's all dark and threatening.

Dammit.

After raising my lantern high, I take a stance and hold out my crystal like a wand. Then I recite to the universe:

"Follow a path filled with love and peace,

Walk in the sunlight with hope and ease.

Walk in the moonlight with unending grace,

Illuminate to help find you in your current place."

The energy from the crystal shoots out like static and illuminates the first alley. Little sparks of energy sizzle in front of me as I follow the lighted path. The tall buildings that are bathed in a bluish light, add to the mystery of this place. I continue traveling down one alley and up the next. I keep searching.

Rach, I'm right behind you. Wait up. Billy's voice is inside my head.

I need to find Melody. She needs my help now. I send my message back.

Billy rushes from behind me and grabs my arm. "Just stop for a minute and think. When you discover them, what will you do? You have no weapon. Only a crystal."

I stare at him blankly. The rest of the Psychic Circle catches up with us.

"There's strength in numbers. It's only Blaine and Melody—his buddies are not with them," Jasmine explains. "We can take him." She opens her fingers to show me her hematite stone.

The group circles in front of me, and each person displays a stone in their open palm. Clarissa carries a blue agate, Deanna holds rose quartz, Billy has hematite, and Sofie shows her green agate. Jimmy displays his amethyst.

I break into a smile. "Thanks, we got this, guys."

I raise my arm to shake Billy's hand loose. "Well, I don't want to lose them. Let's go." The gang follows me down the alley and up the next one. At the end is a cul-de-sac. No way out. A stone bench lines the curb, and I squint to see Melody perched on the edge with her head in her hands. The light from my wand illuminates her upper body. Then I rush over to make sure she's okay.

"Mel?" I place my hands on her arms. She peers up at my face in a stare. Her glassy eyes - all teary, and her body trembling. "Where's Blaine, honey?"

"Who? ... Um... he went to bring me some water. I was ready to pass out," she mumbles and licks her lips. She sweeps a hand across her forehead to wipe the droplets of sweat.

Jimmy steps up. "Mel, we need to get you out of here. He's no good. He's hurting you."

Mel stares past Jimmy.

Turning back at the noise of movement in the gravel, I notice Billy pushing a cart up the alley toward us. "Where'd you get that?"

"It was over there at the end of the passage, so I snagged it." Billy pushes it right up to Mel. Then he turns to Jimmy. "Help me get her in it."

Between the two of them, the boys lift Melody and lay her in the wheelbarrow on top of a large burlap bag. She seems really out of it. As a group, we all rush toward the parking lot, pushing that thing in front of us. Billy grabs his keys off the valet board while the boys wedge Mel into the back seat with Jimmy. She slumps over onto Jimmy's lap and once Billy and I climb in; we hit the locks on the doors. He starts the engine as we wave goodbye to the others in our group. They will return to the party on foot, per our plan.

After we pull away from the cars, we approach the winding road near the carousel. I turn my head to glance out the window and spot Blaine running up to the car. "It's Blaine—step on it!" We take off with our tires squealing down the driveway like a bat out of hell and continue speeding onto the main highway and into the night.

Chapter 20

ESCAPE

"Where do we take her?" Billy asks me, his voice noticeably quivering.

I shrug my shoulders and turn to peek in the back seat. Jimmy holds Mel's head with one hand and strokes her hair with the other. He raises his head to meet me. Tears are pooling in his eyes and begin falling down his cheeks. Visibly, Jimmy is a wreck. This really is taking a toll on him.

"Is she breathing?" I ask him.

"Yes, thank God. I will kill that bastard if anything else happens to her." He sniffs and continues smoothing her hair. Mel is totally out of it.

"Well, we can't bring her to your house, Rach. It's the first spot Blaine would look for her." Billy's death grip on the steering wheel has me concerned as he sorts it all out.

Jimmy tugs on my shoulder. "Drive us to my place. Nobody knows where I live except you two."

"Good idea," I agree, as I put my hand on his for reassurance.

We all swerve to the right as Billy makes a sharp turn onto the Boulevard and a left onto Mountain Ave. About 200 feet down, we veer down Jimmy's street. His house sits at the end of the block at the cul-de-sac. The lights are off, and the building is dark. The gray-colored bi-level waits for us near a four-car asphalt driveway. Billy turns the car and parks beside the garage. He pulls out the key and rests his head on the steering wheel with a deep exhale.

Billy looks toward Jimmy. "Nobody's home?"

"No worries. I have a key. My parents and my sister are visiting my grandma in New York City. They'll be home tomorrow. We'll use the back door. Help me with Melody."

Billy grabs her legs and Jimmy carries her upper body. For such a serious situation, it's comical to watch the boys juggle Melody as they walk, trying not to drop her. She is still unconscious.

We navigate the slate walkway around to the rear of the house, past the picnic table to the sliding doors. Jimmy steadies Mel and hands me his keys. As soon as I open the door, the guys manage to bring Melody inside and lay her on the blue couch in the den. I lift her head to slide a pillow underneath and smooth out the fabric of her black gown. Jimmy turns the switch on the small white lamp on the end table.

"Jimmy, can you bring some water for Mel when she wakes up? And do you have a washcloth I can dampen and put on her forehead?" I ask.

"Sure." He disappears into the kitchen.

Billy's arm slides across my back, and he lays his head next to mine on my shoulder. "You know, you're amazing. Despite all the shit she's done to you, you still want help. That's why I love you."

My heartbeat grows loud in my ears. "It's not her fault Blaine is manipulating her. We have to help her. We have to figure this out."

Jimmy gives me a wet cloth in a small bowl after returning with a bottle of water. "Here you go." He sinks to the floor near the couch next to her head. He whispers in her ear, "Mel, you'll be all right now. You're with us. You're safe." Then he gently takes her hand and cradles it in his.

I reach over, push her hair back off her face, and place the wet washcloth across her forehead. She feels almost feverish, so maybe this will help. Looking down at Jimmy's hand wrapped around hers, I notice she has one of those stupid binding bracelets, like the thing we cut off of Billy's wrist, not too long ago.

Billy notices what I am staring at, pulls out his pocketknife, and flips it open. "I'll take care of that." He slides the blade under the string and slices it off Mel's wrist. The beads scatter everywhere. "Good riddance." Billy walks over to the wall and bangs on it with his fists, letting off some steam.

In the meantime, I take out the protection pouch I had slipped into my leather bag tied to my belt. "I'm going to tie this to Melody so it will keep her safe from Blaine's clutches." I proceed to tie the thin straps to her bra strap and stuff it down the bodice of her gown. "There, that should keep her safe."

As Mel wakes up, I place my hand on the side of her face. "Hey honey, you're safe. You're okay," I reassure her. She licks her lips and tries to find her voice.

"Give her some water," Jimmy says and hands me the bottle off of the end table. After a few sips, she attempts to sit up but falls right down.

"Take a few minutes to rest," I tell her. Then I excuse myself to use the bathroom, leaving Jimmy a few moments alone with Mel. She closes her eyes and he continues to caress her hand.

I wave Billy over toward the kitchen so that he leaves the room, too. He reaches over, locks the sliding doors, and pulls the drapes closed before he follows me out of the room. After my brief pee break, Billy is waiting for me in the kitchen.

"What are we gonna do about this whole shit show?" I ask in a hushed voice.

Billy grasps my shoulders and searches my face. "To save her, we'll need to bring it to the high witch council. It's the only way to stop that bastard."

"But won't they ban Melody, too?"

"Maybe not, if we can prove Blaine is the one manipulating everyone, including her."

I hear a noise behind us and turn around quickly to observe Jimmy standing in the doorway, holding Mel, who is presently standing. She's barefoot and her gown is draped over her feet. Her new shoes were tossed by the side of the couch.

"Did you guys hear all of that?" I ask them. The two of them shake their heads, 'Yes.'

"Oh, boy." I jump at the loud crack of thunder that sounds like it is right over the house. The sky lights up in a flash through the windows.

"But you hit the nail on the head," Jimmy says. "It's the only way to stop Blaine." He squeezes Mel's arm.

"I agree, too, now that I can think clearly. I know you're right," Melody concurs. The color comes back to her complexion.

I move forward and give my old friend a big hug. She buries her face in my hair. "We just have to figure out when and where. Then we pray there is no retaliation."

Chapter 21

AMBUSHED

It's Wednesday, and that god-awful, end-of-day bell is ringing. It's hurting my ears. Thankfully, we have the next two days off, so the maintenance guys can disinfect the school. The superintendent has given us a few additional days off because of the Covid pandemic. It's a great idea to air out the school to get rid of the germs and give it a thorough cleaning. I'm looking forward to giving the school rat race and the latest drama a rest.

I tumble the numbers on my lock and swing the locker door open, a little too enthusiastically. It crashes against the locker next to me. Oops! The teachers are giving us a brief break–no homework for once. Yay. My backpack will be ultra-light today. I stuff my gym shirt and shorts in the pack, along with a bottle of water and a couple of snack bars off the top shelf. Then I re-set the lock and join the moving crowd, shuffling down the hallway. At the last minute, I decide to duck into the girl's bathroom for a pit stop before I exit.

Once in the stall, I lift my shirt over my head, changing from my school clothes into my gym clothes. It's 80 degrees today and I want to take advantage of the wonderful weather we've been having by going for a run through the backwoods. I could use a good stretch, and I rarely get the chance.

Tossing my pack over my shoulder, I wash my hands, pat them dry, and head out the door. Then, I mentally contact Billy, so he knows my plans–*Hey Billy, I'm going for a run right after school through the woods behind the school.*

Hi Babe–Okay. See you later tonight, he responds.

Smiling to myself, I make sure I tuck my phone in the side pocket of my pack, and it's all zipped up.

Once assured that I have everything I need, I begin my jog along the dirt path past the bleachers.

I notice the birds are extra noisy today, with their chirping and chattering much louder than usual. So, I stop for a moment, pull out my phone, and put in my earbuds to drown them out. After clicking on my favorite music app, I secure the phone back in the side pocket and continue on my way. Starting slower at first, I increase my speed a notch to feel the burn and settle into a steady rhythm.

After a while, I glance up and see that the sun's a little lower in the sky than it was when I started running, so I check my watch. I've been running for about an hour. After gradually slowing down, I slide onto the wooden bench along the path for a brief rest. I fall back against the frame and take out my water bottle for a long swig, wipe my face with my shirt, and decide to lean back and close my eyes, calming my breathing down. My legs feel like jelly. Ugh.

Suddenly, my muscles tense up on their own. Beads of sweat form on my upper lip and across my forehead. A weird foreboding energy surrounds me. My eyes blink open to see figures in black hoodies all around me. Confusion clouds my head with unfamiliar faces. I panic and begin kicking as hard as I can, and I am surprised by the hand coming at my face from behind me. The hand, wrapped in a handkerchief, latches onto my nose and mouth. A strange smell from it has me woozy.

"We got her" is all I hear as my vision goes from blurry to black in seconds.

Lights out.

* * *

The next thing I know, there's fog clouding my brain. I lift myself up on one elbow and realize my wrists are bound in front of me with a red bandana. Closing my eyes and trying to concentrate, I try to figure out where I am and what is happening here. But to no avail. The darkness has settled in, and I lay my head back down with a clunk on what I think is cold concrete.

A rustling noise coming from the other end of the room wakes me, but everything is dark as coal and I can't see a thing. I have no idea how long I've been out, but I am not on the bare concrete anymore. Instead, a scratchy blanket under me rubs against my cheek. My hands are still bound tight, and my ankles are raw and bound, too.

What the hell is going on here?

I can decipher the sound of footsteps padding down several stairs toward the space I now occupy.

A door knob clicks, and I pick up on the distinguishable sound of a door unlocking before it gets pushed open. I shut my eyes tight to feign sleep. It's my best course of action right now. The voices sound masculine, and I can make out bits and pieces of the conversation.

"Master B. seems pleased. We did a great job. What do we do with her now?"

"I know what I want to do with her," says another voice with an evil laugh.

"Easy now, tiger. You don't want to get on his bad side. He's doing this for that bitch, Melody. He thinks he's doing her a favor. We do the job right, get paid, and get the hell out. We just have to make sure she stays alive."

The ground vibrates as the first guy approaches me. He throws a blanket over me, dragging it against my arm. Then he touches my wrist, probably checking if I have a pulse.

"Is she okay?" the partner asks.

"Yes," he grunts.

With this, the footsteps retreat, the door gets pulled open, and a lock clicks shut. The silence pervades for several minutes, and when the coast is clear, I open my eyes. Blackness surrounds me.

Good, at least the sheet is over my body, not my head.

My racing heart pounds against my rib cage as I breathe in through my nose and out through my mouth in a feeble attempt to slow down the race. The dampness tickles my nose. But, after many tries, my breath is a little calmer.

Mustering up all the internal energy I can, I push a call out to Billy using our telepathic connection. *Billy, I need you. Can you hear me? I'm in trouble.*

I wait calmly for his answer, trying to be patient. In the interim, I try to wiggle my arms free. The bandana seems to loosen as I wiggle and twist, trying to contort my hand into a narrow bundle to slide through the knotted fabric.

Rach, where are you? I hear his message loud and clear.

Oh my God, Billy. Thank you. I don't know where I am.

Well, what happened to you?

So, I tell him my story... *I went for a run after school and some guys dressed in all black surrounded me. One held me from behind with something on a rag that made me pass out.*

Are you okay? The concern in his voice bleeds through his telepathic message.

I think so. It feels like I am in a basement room. It has a concrete floor. And I know Blaine is involved.

That bastard! He sends his thoughts out.

I cringe when I think of the time he caught Blaine at the Medieval Fair. If I didn't calm Billy down, I swear, I think he would have severely injured Blaine. Back then, he said something like… if I ever catch you again, I will kill you.

I try to change the subject. *So how can we figure out my location?*

It doesn't work. I can sense his agitation.

Do you have any idea where Blaine lives? Billy asks.

No… but wait… He has a sister that lives in town. Mel told me that her name was Kathy Kean.

Ok, I'll try to see if we can get a street address on her. Hang tight. I'll let you know what I find out. I love you, he says.

This sounds like the set-up for a TV Horror miniseries, and they rarely end well.

Chapter 22

RESCUE ME

A patch of kaleidoscopic light appears on the floor next to my bound wrists as a soft breeze flips up the corner of the curtain on a basement window I didn't notice before. The glass is either open or broken. My wiggling has loosened the knot on the bandana around my wrists, so I raise it to my mouth and gnaw on it with my teeth. It's working!

Rach, I hear in my head.

Oh my God, Billy. Any luck?

After pulling at the last taut piece of the knot, it releases, and the bandana drops, freeing my hands.

I wince and rub at the marks left behind on my skin.

Yes, he tells me telepathically. *I got Sofie to look up Blaine's sister's address on the psychic store's mailing list. Kathy frequents that store. Hopefully, he took you to her house. No stone unturned, right? I'm going to check it out now.*

My heart offers a little jig right about now. *Okay, let me know. I hope that's where I am.*

Hope is a wonderful thing.

I close my eyes and pray, calling aloud to God to please listen to my prayer. Afterward, I mentally call out to each member of the Psychic Circle. Our practices of connecting with each other's energy might finally pay off, and they'll catch my telepathic message. I reach out to Jasmine and Clarissa and wait a few minutes for their feedback.

Nothing.

Then I try two more members, *Sofie and Deanna — can you guys hear me? I'm in trouble and need your help.* Then I wait again.

Nothing.

Jimmy—can you hear me? I push out with all the energy I can drum up. Another waiting game. Then I fold my hands in prayer. *Please, please, please let them find me,* I say.

Rachel, is that you? Jimmy's voice returns, loud and clear.

"Yes!" I proceed to tell him what's going on.

Optimism fills my heart. I push myself up to a sitting position and work to untie my feet. Once free, I attempt to stand and shuffle over to that window. Success! When I pull the curtain back, the house next door is visible through the broken glass. When I put my eye up to the corner of the window, all I see is red brick. Then, I twist my head and focus my attention on the curb - the number on the mailbox is 15.

Excitement bubbles up in my chest as I mentally call out to Jimmy. *Hey, I can see out the basement window. The neighbor's house is red brick with the number 15 on the mailbox. Guess it means this house has to be 13 or 17. Please meet up with Billy and tell him. I need you two to rescue me.*

Okay, I'll do that.

At that moment, a shadow blocks out the light coming through the window, and I fall backward onto my butt. *Ouch.* I grapple to stand up again. As I look up, I see Melody's face peering through the broken glass.

"Oh my God, Rachel. Are you okay?" Melody whispers.

"What?" I am confused. "Is Blaine with you?"

"No, he's not here. I got your telepathic SOS. What has he done to you?"

"Mel, is this part of your little trap?" I'm not certain if I can trust her.

"Shh... listen," Melody replies softly as she looks from side to side. "Something is happening with Blaine—like he's Dr. Jekyll and Mr. Hyde. He's still got a powerful hold on me. I can't shake it. He makes me do things against my will. I know I am perpetually under a spell when I am near him." She gets closer to the windowsill. "His friends will come back with food for you. Unlock the window latch, and I'll see if I can pull you out."

I hesitate for a moment. I want to trust my old best friend.

"Now!" she urges.

I reach up and flip the lock open. When pushing the window back, the broken glass skitters to the floor. Next, I drag a chair to the wall and climb up. It's a snug fit. "I don't know about this."

"It's the only way," Mel replies. She reaches for my arms and tugs at me.

I wiggle and contort my body to conform to the small opening. Okay, I'm past my hips now. She gently tries to yank a little harder, and I tumble onto Mel as my sneakers clear the opening. I'm out.

I spot Jimmy and Billy running up the driveway. They both grab for Melody to pull her away from me.

"No." I yell. "Mel has helped me to escape. It was Blaine and his friends that kidnapped me, not her." I pull myself up and brush off my pants.

"What?" Billy spits out and he lets her go. Then Jimmy releases her too.

"No time to explain the details. Where's your car?" I stare at Billy, and he points across the street.

"They'll return any minute. Let's go." Melody tugs on my arm. We all run over to the car, jump in, and take off. I lay back on the seat and close my eyes, trying not to hyperventilate. Melody is sprawled out in the backseat with me.

"You're bleeding," she says as she takes out a tissue, blots the blood on my hand, and wipes the blood from my knee.

"Probably from the broken glass," I reply.

Billy drives us to my house, where we all exit the car and run around the rear of the house. We practically fly through the patio door, and I turn the deadbolt shut. Scrambling down the stairs, we pile into the basement rec room.

I drop to the floor, crisscrossing my legs, my head resting in my arms on the old sea chest, trying to catch my breath. Billy's right beside me, rubbing my back. I glance up at Jimmy and Mel on the couch, holding each other's hands. We all sit here in the dark, not saying a word for about 15 long minutes. Silence is golden.

Come on, get it together, I tell myself. Billy smiles and pats my shoulder.

The conversation turns to Blaine and his supposed plan. Melody confides in us and explains how Blaine is always controlling her every move, like a puppet. When she's away from him, she has clarity, but ever since the whole Midsummer Night's Dream Ball event, she fears for her life. She doesn't know what to do.

"Mel, how did you catch my telepathic messages? I didn't realize you could do that."

She stares at me with tears in her eyes. "You and I have a very special close connection. It's been a while now since I've been practicing my skill. It's a talent I've had since I was a kid, which stems from another lifetime. At least that's where I think it comes from. I realize I can hear Jimmy's thoughts, too." She turns and squeezes his hand.

Jimmy's face lights up. "Yes, I feel we have some sort of connection, too. I've even seen you in my dreams before. It's eerie."

Chapter 23

SEVEN DIFFERENT KINDS OF WRONG

Although we did nothing wrong, we sit here cowering in the darkness for what seems like an eternity in fear of being discovered. I realize that I'm holding my breath in case the littlest sound gives away our presence. I blow it out slowly.

Something outside draws our attention. The moon, so large and bright, casts its rays through the windows and the curtains in a hazy silver glow.

After three knocks on the door, it stops, then three more knocks. That's the signal.

I get up to unlatch the deadbolt, and Jasmine, Clarissa, Deanna, and Sofie tumble inside. I click it closed again.

"We got your SOS. Sorry, it took everyone so long," Jasmine says as she hugs me.

Clarissa steps out from behind her. "Glad you're okay. We drove by the address and saw Blaine's car parked in the driveway of his sister's house. They are still there."

"Don't worry, they did not follow us," Sofie adds as she looks around the room. Her eyes stop at Melody. She raises her hand and points. "What's she doing here?"

"If you come in, I can explain." I explain the details of what transpired during my 'kidnapping' and tell them how Melody rescued me. I think I've convinced the three of them to help Melody. Sofie is still holding out.

"You're out of your mind," yells Sofie in my direction, clenching her fists. "After all she has done to you and Billy!"

I get up off the couch. "Let's just be civil, okay? We will bring the whole thing to the High Witch Council and see what they decide to do. Blaine is the manipulator here, and he obviously has Melody under his spell. If we can prove it, then they will ban him instead of her.

Sofie stands up too. "And what about the subject of the spell book that we all tiptoe around? What about that? What are you planning on doing with it? Not so innocent now." She smirks as she sits back down.

Melody leans forward on the couch cushion. "Can I say something here?"

"Go ahead." My hand is on her knee.

"In retrospect, I know I am not innocent in a lot of these situations. Some things I regret doing when I wasn't under Blaine's influence, and I am truly sorry for that. But I never intended to hurt any of you. At one time, you were all my friends. If you can find it in your heart to give me back the spell book, I will bury it, and you'll never hear about it again. All of those spells passed down from my family are irreplaceable."

Static energy makes the hairs stand up on my arms as it circles the room. I rub them down with my fingers. "Come on, guys, we're getting all riled up. I sense it in the air and you can as well. Let's stop for a few minutes." I suggest.

Billy just shakes his head.

I step over to my mom's herbal cabinet and open up the bottom drawer where I stashed her book the last time we used it. Pulling out the spell book, I walk over to Mel and extend my hand to her. "This is yours." I give her the book. "It's yours again, in good faith."

Melody accepts it and gives me a side hug. "Thank you, Rach. I promise you'll never see it again."

"Okay. I don't want the police involved in the kidnapping situation. The elders can take care of Blaine's punishment," I admit to the group.

Sofie stands up. "Do what you want, Rachel. She won't be part of the Psychic Circle again if I have anything to do with it. She rushes over to the patio door and lets herself out.

"Shit," Billy spits out. "That was seven different kinds of wrong."

I close my eyes for a moment to center myself. Then I rise, moving toward the door. Before latching it, I say, "Mel, I think you should leave now so everyone can calm down. We'll let you know when we are ready to talk to the council."

Melody nods as she gets up quietly and makes her way over to me. I hug her and whisper in her ear, "Thank you for saving me." She steps out, and I lock the door behind her.

Unfortunately, that didn't turn out as I hoped it would.

Chapter 24

FREE THE SOUL

A loud snort startles me, making me sit up straight in the recliner. Thump. My paperback falls from my lap to the floor. My goodness, that's me. I immersed myself in reading a book about crystal grids and must have dozed off. LOL, I guess I really do snore. I chuckle to myself a little.

The moonlight streams through the open blind in the living room, as the time on the digital clock near the television reads 11:11 pm. That magic number again. A stale scent of my patchouli incense lingers in the air.

In the doorway, a hazy figure is moving toward me.

"Mom, is that you?" I call out, softly. *Why am I whispering?*

No answer.

As the fuzzy outline approaches me, it stops right by the coffee table. My eyes blink and I try to focus. I can see it better now. Now I recognize him, Mr. Payne, Mel's dad. The spiked blonde hair, blue eyes, and telltale smile give him away.

"Hello, Rachel," the spirit says to me.

"Hi, Mr. Payne." He has visited me a few times before.

"Time is getting away from you. You must help Melody clear her karma."

"We are helping. Our group has let the Witch Council intervene and have them reprimand Blaine. Once we tell them all about how this guy is controlling Mel, they will ban him and make him pay."

"I know, I've seen. Don't delay, I am here to warn you. If you don't move forward immediately, we may lose her to the dark side forever. You need to help free Mel's soul. Please, swear to me you will." Mr. Payne's apparition goes fuzzy and starts snapping in and out of focus.

"We promise." There is a loud pop when I reach out to him. Then he disappears. With that, icy coldness fills the void and I remember to breathe again.

I click on the table lamp next to me and scan the room with my eyes. Yes, he's gone. Leaning over to grab my fallen book, my hand shakes on its way back up. I wasn't nervous at all during my visitation from Mr. Payne, but now, I'm a nervous wreck. I promised him we'd help free Melody's soul. Can that really be done? I'll have to deal with that in the morning. I think it's way out of my league.

After washing my face and brushing my teeth, I climb onto my bed and pull the sheet up to my chin. I don't feel the slightest bit tired. Since I had a catnap with my book, I guess it is enough for a second wind. After tossing and turning, I know sleep won't happen, so I give up.

I slide out of bed, grab my phone, and move over to my purple fuzzy chair. Then I tap the numbers on my phone. Billy, usually up until midnight, picks up after two rings.

"Hi, beautiful," he says. That just melts my heart.

"Hi, handsome."

"Everything okay?"

"Yeah, I can't sleep."

"Bummer."

"I want to spend time with you."

"Okay. How about we go for a walk?"

"Sure. Meet me in front of my house in about 10 minutes. I have lots to tell."

"Will do."

I hang up the phone and pull on my jogging pants and a rock & roll tee. Then I sneak out the front door and head down the steps to the driveway.

Billy's already there and waiting. He's so quick. He entwines his fingers with mine as we walk down the sidewalk. The dirt path at the end of the road leads to a big sandpit. Still holding hands, we run down the dusty drive, pulling each other along. Pebbles kick up at our heels. Very impressive enormous boulders that look like a giant tossed them onto the sand are standing guard on either side of the gravel entrance.

We stop, and Billy pulls me up to climb up the first group of rocks with him. We clamber to the top and rest on the flat face. Still hand-in-hand, he leans in to kiss me. It's heavenly. I run my tongue along his as he explores my mouth, tenderly and rhythmically. We both enjoy every second.

We peer up at the moon and the beautiful night sky as we cuddle. I break the silence. "I want you to know I had a visit tonight from Mel's father's spirit."

Billy lets go of our embrace. It seems anything that has to do with Melody still affects him. "What did he want?"

I tell Billy of the details of my visitation and of the promise I made to Mr. Payne to help free her soul.

Like now.

"Did you mention to him about our plan to go to the Council?"

"Yes. We'll have to be sure to tell Silver about it, so she can set this meeting up as soon as she can."

I close my eyes and let out a sigh, rubbing my hands on my pants. I'm worrying myself sick about this ugly situation.

Billy senses it and slides his arm around my shoulder. "It'll be okay. I think it is the right thing to do. The only way to stop Blaine."

I lay my head back against his shoulder. "I hope to God you are right."

Chapter 25

LOVE YOU FOREVER

My Art class ends in about 5 minutes. I slouch in my seat with my arm slung over the back of the chair, taking a deep, satisfied breath. A warm, fuzzy feeling overcomes me.

Meet me in the library during Study Hall. I hear in my head. A message from my boyfriend. No surprise, I am all warm and fuzzy. As an empath, I am picking up his feelings too.

Okay, see you next period, babe. I wonder what's going on now.

The bell rings and I rush down the corridor to Study Hall. I need to get a pass to the library with an excuse to work on a project. *That was too easy.*

Hurrying down the second hallway, I breathe in deeply and smell the scent of all those books as I turn into the library entrance. It hits you all at once. Yes, I'm just a closet book nerd. It's one of my favorite things to do. There is nothing like smelling a physical book.

Billy is waving to me from a corner table in the back of the room. I spot Jimmy next to him. Darn, I guess it's not a romantic rendezvous. Their chuckling reaches me as I approach the table. They are in good spirits.

I toss my backpack on the empty chair next to Billy. Then I bend down to plant my lips on his for a smooch.

"Hi," I say to Jimmy as I look his way. "What's going on, you two?"

Billy answers, "Jimmy wanted to meet with us. He's had another dream."

I sit forward on the edge of my seat. "Do tell."

Jimmy leans in and whispers, "Well, this time, it was very vivid. It started where it left off before, with a vision of 10-year-old me and 10-year-old Melody. We both were wearing Lakota buckskin attire with fringe and beads. In the dream, we're involved in a ritual, kneeling on deer hide, facing each other, and holding hands. Lit candles were flickering on a small piece of log in the middle of a teepee, making shadows dance on the walls. We promised to love each other forever. I could hear our vows as if I was there. Then Melody inserted the tip of her knife in my thumb, far enough to produce a small bead of blood. I did the same to her."

"That's a real blood ritual!" I say.

"Yep," Jimmy continues, "Pressing our two thumbs together, we twisted them to mix our blood. Then, we each licked off the blood from our thumbs. The metallic taste lingered on my tongue. A quick kiss on the lips and the ceremony was done. We were officially blood partners at 10 years old."

"Wow, no wonder you are so compelled to help her." I place my hand on top of Jimmy's.

"Holy crap. Do you really love her?" Billy asks him.

Jimmy takes a deep breath and blows it out. He lowers his eyes to the table. "Yes, I do. I mean, I hardly know her in this lifetime, but I feel like I've known her forever. And I guess I have."

"Come with us to the council. Your presence there will help. We're meeting at the bookstore after school.

Walk over there with us. Melody will need your support." I try to convince him how important it is.

Jimmy folds his hands in front of him on his notebook and shuts his eyes for a moment. "I'll be there. This is part of my destiny."

I look from Billy to Jimmy. "Here is what I am thinking — Mel is meeting me beforehand. To appear more innocent and less threatening, I will help her remove all that black goth makeup and nail polish."

"Great idea." Billy lays his hand on my arm. "That's why I love you. You are so smart."

"Thanks. I think it will help her case."

"Can you possibly have her put on something different than her usual black clothes from head to toe," Jimmy adds. "Dress her in something colorful and happy."

"Got it." I nod.

The bell rings, the period is over.

As we stand up, I turn to them. "Let's hope this works. See you later, guys."

"Cross your fingers!"

Chapter 26

SWEET AND INNOCENT

It's the beginning of June and the sun shines brightly in all its glory. I find myself staring out the window in a daze, watching the cardinals resting in the apple tree outside my bedroom window.

The doorbell rings, and I can hear Mom rushing toward the front door.

"Honey, I'll get it," Mom yells up the stairs. I can hear her unlock the door and swing it open.

"Thanks, Mom," I call down.

"Oh, Melody! So nice to see you. It's been a long time. How have you been, sweetheart?" Mom gives her an enormous hug as she enters the threshold. I can see them from the top of the stairs. "Rachel, it's Melody."

"Send her up, Mom. Thanks." I go back to my room.

It's been a very long time since Melody has been to our house, long before she was out of the Psychic Circle. But, since she saved me from my kidnappers, I feel I can trust her again.

Mel stops at my bedroom doorway and knocks three times on the woodwork. I look up. She stands there in all her black-colored glory.

"Hey." I stand up and pull her into the room. "It's been a while since you've been here."

"I know."

"This is a tremendous step for you," I say. "I mean, in joining us before the Council."

"It certainly is." She fiddles with her rings, spinning them around her fingers. Her voice quivers a little. "This needs to be done. I totally understand."

I nod.

We continue heading toward my desk, and I motion for Melody to sit down.

Opening the drawer, I take out my makeup remover, blue eyeshadow, pink lipstick, and blush, and place them in front of Melody on the desk.

She looks up at me inquisitively. "What's all this for?" Mel asks.

An awkward moment. *How do I tell her?*

"Well... I talked with the boys, and we discussed how we should prepare you for approaching the Witch Council. We all decided that it will be beneficial to everyone if we change your makeup and clothes to help your case—you need to trust me on this."

She studies me for a moment, then looks down at the makeup. "I'm not so sure about this, but I do trust you. So go ahead."

I take the makeup remover pads and swipe them over Mel's eyes. It takes several minutes and several makeup remover cloths to wipe off all the black stuff from her eyes and lashes, but with a little perseverance and some scrubbing, I have a blank canvas. I don't think I've ever seen Mel without makeup, except in my visions. With the blue eye shadow and pink lipstick, this girl looks nothing like the Goth queen that just walked in here ten minutes ago.

Adding a teensy bit of lip gloss, I ask Mel to rub her lips together. It smells heavenly.

"Now, let's pick out something nice to wear." I pull her over to my closet. "How about this?" I hold up a cute denim skirt and a daisy print top.

Melody shakes her head 'no', as I shake my head 'yes'.

"Just try it on. Trust me."

Melody takes off her black corset top and leather skirt, then tosses them on the chair. The black boots come off too. I hold out the skirt and she shimmies into it. After sliding the top off the hanger, I help to get it over her head.

"One more thing before you stand in front of the mirror." I grab the heated curling iron to make a few curls in her poker-straight black hair, curling the hair away from her face. *What a difference!*

"I hope you guys are right about this," Melody sounds hopeful as she walks toward the floor-length mirror. "Oh, wow!" She leans forward to inspect her transformation with twinkling eyes.

"You look positively beautiful." I put my hands on her shoulders. "Own it!"

Mel closes her eyes for a moment to compose herself and stares at me through the mirror. "It's not my style at all, but I understand what you're trying to accomplish, and I love you for it. I look like a very different person."

"Sweet and innocent, right? That's what I was going for. This is perfect."

Mel shoots me a model smile.

"Oh, do you have that protection pouch with you?" I ask before we leave.

She reaches into her backpack and pulls out the little black pouch.

"Perfect. Tie it to your bra strap as I did before and tuck it into your top. It will provide much-needed protection from Blaine since we cut off that bracelet last month."

"Okay, let's do this," I say as I unplug the curling iron and choose a pair of denim wedges to complete the look. "Here you go." She puts the shoes on, then I grab her hand as we walk out the door.

"Wish us luck."

Chapter 27

AND HARM NONE

As we walk up Main Street on our way to the Psychic Connection, the sky is gray and overcast, and I can see that the sign in the front window says 'closed'. The gang is huddled up together by the side of the building.

"Hi, guys. What's going on?" I say as I point to the sign.

"They closed the store early for our meeting," Sofie tells us. "Standard protocol."

"Where's Melody?" Billy asks.

I knew they wouldn't recognize her. I pulled off a wonderful transformation. Tugging on Mel's arm, I pull her in front of me. "Right here."

All I can hear are their gasps.

"Holy crap, Melody–it's you!" Clarissa reaches out to touch her arm.

"Wow," Sofie adds.

Jimmy takes her hand. "You're beautiful!"

"Sorry, I didn't recognize you," Billy apologizes. He is acting civil for once.

I wonder where Jasmine and Deanna are? I notice they are absent from the group today.

"Jasmine's grandmother is so sick that they both visited her to help," Billy whispers to me. I guess he heard what I was thinking.

The side door creaks and Silver's head emerges as she beckons us over. "Come on in. They are ready for you."

In a single file, we walk through the store and down the stairs to the meeting room. Stale air tickles my nose. Someone staged the room differently today. The two Elders we met last time are waiting at a long table on a platform at the head of the room. They are wearing their long black cloaks. When they see us, they both reach up and push the hoods off their heads. The first witch wears a mess of wavy gray hair. The other one has shoulder-length, sleek black hair pulled into a low ponytail. A man with the blackest of eyes joins them, clothed in a deep purple cape and long, wavy salt and pepper hair.

Sofie walks towards the left of the room to sit with Silver. The rest of us file in the row behind them. I hold hands with Mel to make sure that she sits next to me. Over in the opposite row, I spot Blaine with three sidekicks from his gang. All four are oblivious to us or intentionally ignoring us. I am guessing the latter.

Silver, the store owner, lights three rather large candles placed in front of the Elders on the bench with long-stemmed matches. In front of the candles, a colorful abalone shell holds a pleasant-smelling smoldering incense with hints of patchouli and sandalwood. The scent is very calming.

The Elder named Edith bangs a gavel. "We must adhere to a few rules before we start this meeting. Only one person can talk at a time. Only when asked a question may you interrupt the one talking. If you break these rules, we will ask you to leave." She means business.

The man in the purple attire slowly rises. "I am Luther." He motions to the other two witches, "And this is Edith and Helga, whom you have met with before. We are here to take care of an infraction made against the treaty that was made recently. It warned that the council would punish any retribution taken."

I squeeze Melody's hand between us for support.

He continues... "The accepted agreement set aside boundaries for each of the groups involved. It assigned the stone circle east of the store for meditations and Psychic Circle gatherings. The local coven was to use the area to the west of the store for their meetings. The treaty forbade anyone from disturbing or spying on either group during their rituals." Silence hung in the atmosphere after his voice stopped reverberating. "Retribution has reared its ugly head, and Sofie and Silver brought the infraction report to this council."

Helga clears her throat. "Will Melody Payne please rise and stand before this tribunal?"

I squeeze Mel's hand again before she stands up and approaches the Elders. She taps her chest, signaling me she has her protection pouch on her.

"Miss Payne, the report states you are also a victim in all of this. Please tell us about it," Edith asks.

Melody speaks slowly and clearly, "Blaine Mills has controlled me against my will. He cast a spell on me. My friends can attest to this. While we were carrying out these horrible acts, I was being completely manipulated by him."

I raise my hand.

"Yes?" the man acknowledges me.

"I am one of her friends. Can I add to that?"

"Please approach the Elders."

I rise and stand beside Melody at the front. "My name is Rachel Wells, and I can attest to Melody being under Blaine's spell. Her eyes were always glassy, and she was incoherent much of the time. It seemed as if she was his puppet. Melody was not acting like herself at all. I've known her a long time, and Blaine certainly has a hold on her. When she was away from Blaine, she returned to her normal self." I look back at my friends, and they are all nodding in agreement. I squeeze Mel's hand and smile at her.

"Thank you. Miss Wells and Miss Payne, you may sit down."

The warlock looks toward the other group. "Blaine Mills, please approach the Tribunal."

Blaine gets up to stand in front of the Elders.

"Mr. Mills, we have already met with you in private, along with your parents, and discussed what was in the reports. We have decided your fate." Blaine hangs his head down. "That's right, you should be ashamed of your actions. Miss Edith, please read the verdict." The man passes the paper to her.

Blaine, wringing his hands, looks like he is having trouble keeping his body from trembling.

"Mr. Mills, this Tribunal finds you guilty of 2 infractions against the original agreement and one additional count of retribution. We ban you from this store and its grounds. In addition, you will be on probation with our coven for 1 year. During that year, this council will bind you from using your powers. Please stay after this meeting and we will bind you today. At the end of the year's time, we may re-evaluate your situation. Do not think of any reprisals because we will monitor your activities. It is done. You may sit back down." Miss Edith passes the paper to Miss Helga.

Blaine shuffles back to his chair and sinks down in a slump. *Ha, not such a big man anymore,* I think to myself. A little chuckle comes from Billy.

"Melody Payne, although you were an accessory to some of these infractions, you were determined to be unknowingly under Mr. Mill's spell, so we will not ban you from the store. However, we will put you on probation with our coven for 3 months. We met with your mother earlier, and we notified her of our decision." With that, Luther hits the gavel and all three Elders rise and part the curtain behind them. They wave Blaine to follow them so they can perform the binding. The door there leads to a secret room.

"Thank you all for coming," Silver says, as she guides us up the stairs and out of the store.

Again, some serious shit went down. I hear in my mind. Billy is tight-lipped.

You know it, I respond.

Justice was served today.

Chapter 28

WORD ON THE STREET

Stepping out through the sliding patio doors into the backyard, I raise my hand to shelter my eyes from the brilliant sunlight. The billowy clouds sail across the sky in slow motion, allowing the sun to peek through with its bright rays. What a beautiful morning and a perfect summer day! The weatherman is predicting it to be in the low 90s today.

Hey, Sunshine. I hear in my head. Billy starts my day off fine. I smile to myself, as I appreciate my awesome guy.

Hello, back! I convey my thoughts to him telepathically.

Whatcha doing today? He asks.

Why? Have any ideas?

Yeah, let's get together. I have some juicy gossip that I want to share with you in person, babe.

OK, my house or yours? I inquire. There's a pause.

Hey, can we meet in the woods behind the bleachers instead? I'll bring my beach towel like we used to do. I'm liking this one.

Love that. See you there in fifteen. My smile spreads.

I stretch my shoulders by raising my hands toward those clouds. Then I bend over to my right and switch over to the left. *Ah, that feels so good.*

After making my way back inside, I latch the door shut behind me and skip up the stairs. A great start to a wonderful day. I poke my head into my mom's room, where she is sitting in front of the mirror, fixing her unruly brown hair into a messy ponytail for her shift at work today. She's wearing her navy-blue scrubs. Mom's usual schedule is three 12-hour days at the hospital as a charge nurse. The dark rings under her blue eyes are a steady reminder she's been working too much lately by accepting extra shifts, which compromises her sleep.

"Hey Mom," I say as I reach out to smooth down her ponytail. "I hope you have a calm day at work today. Billy and I are thinking of taking a nice long walk." I hug her shoulder.

"Okay, honey," Mom replies and kisses me on the cheek. "I left you some money downstairs."

"See you later, after your shift." I stop at my room, grab my cross-body purse, and hurry down the steps to go meet Billy. I got the ten-dollar bill she left for me on my way out.

I saunter down the trail in the woods alongside the school, then veer left on the path that leads out to the bleachers where Billy is sitting, forming a heart with his thumbs and index fingers for me. Yep, that's my goofy guy! I drop my bag on the bench and slide my arms up around his neck in a hug, turning to press my mouth to his in a tender kiss on those waiting lips. His kiss is so amorous, sending shivers down my spine. It never seems to get old.

"Well, hello to you too," he says between my smooches, as he slides his hands along my waist and onto my butt for a squeeze.

"Oh!" I wasn't expecting that move.

He pulls back for a moment with a sly grin on his face. "I'm glad you like it. Here, sit for a minute. I want to tell you what I heard. You will not believe it."

Sitting down on the bottom bleacher, he pats the spot next to him. I plop down, so intrigued. Unable to fathom what this is all about, I wait with bated breath.

"Word on the street is The Psychic Connection was broken into late last night, and they arrested Blaine for it. The cops took him away in handcuffs. Can you believe it?"

"Holy Crap! What did he steal?" I hold out my hands.

"Some witchcraft ritual supplies and jewelry. Go figure."

I lean back. "He just received his banishment. Sounds like retaliation to me."

Billy puts his hands on my shoulders. "Wait— there's more. They are sending him to juvenile detention since he has so many other marks on his record. And get this... his family put the house up for sale today. They plan on moving across the country to Los Angeles."

"Wow, now that's Karma in action!" I shout, raising my hands high. Billy slaps me five.

He suddenly gets this serious look on his face. "Before we go to our special spot, I need to talk to you." He slides his arm over my back.

"Okay, what?"

He looks me in the eye and says, "You're way too trusting. The circle members, including me, think you are out of your mind by trusting Melody again. After all the shit she pulled, do you still want to give her another chance? We care about you, Rach, so we took an informal vote, and the entire group wants nothing to do with Mel. She is not welcome. She will never be part of the Psychic Circle again." Billy slides his arm off my back and holds my hands instead. "What are you thinking?"

I slip my hands out from under his and rub them on my thighs. I take a deep swallow. "Here's the thing—we were best of friends before everything happened. The Melody I knew is still in there somewhere. She became the victim when Blaine took control of her. It's not her fault. I know I can be too trusting—it's my nature. Deep down in my soul, I'm sure that it's the right thing to do. I want to trust her. She needs to know that. And she hasn't seen Blaine since we clipped her bracelet off." I stand up and take a few steps away from him. I fold my arms over my chest and close my eyes for a moment.

Billy reaches for me, but I stand my ground. He drops his hands and says, "I understand because I know your nature. You would never leave a friend hanging. You are too caring." He moves over behind me and rubs his hands up and down my arms. "But you'll have to mend your relationship alone, without the Psychic Circle. Sorry."

Tears stream down my cheeks and dribble lower into the sides of my mouth. I can't help it. Billy reaches around and snuggles me tight. He extends his thumbs and wipes my tears. At least he understands where I am coming from. "I just want to go home now. We can meditate another time," I say. I pull away from him and begin walking back down the trail.

I hope to GOD that I am making the right decision for all concerned.

Chapter 29

KARMA LIKE THIS

I find myself daydreaming as I stare at the bumblebees buzzing around the perfectly manicured azalea bushes next to the gazebo. I watch as they visit each blossom on this warm and sunny day. Suddenly, a sense of responsibility waves over me and invades my space. Sitting here at the bus stop in front of the town hall, I shake my head. Perhaps it's my spirit guide's way to nudge me into opening up to Melody and divulging the messages that her father has been providing to me during his periodic visitations. I know she is open to stuff like this, and I am hoping it will gain her trust again.

The bus comes to an abrupt halt as I glance up toward the open doors. Melody jumps from the last step to the curb. "Hi, Rach!" The corner of her black hoodie flaps in the wind as she runs over to me, waving her hand as if we haven't seen each other in years.

"Hi, Mel. How was the trip?" I ask as we hug it out.

"Fine, silly. I only live in the next town. It's just a fifteen-minute ride. Good to see you." The old Mel is back. The muscles in my jaw relax. I wasn't too sure which version of Mel would appear.

"My mom is picking us up in about ten minutes. Take a load off." I motion for her to sit on the bench in the quaint gazebo used as a bus stop.

Melody slides out of her jacket and tosses it on top of her backpack on the ground. A smile breaks out on her lips as she catches me staring. "What?" Her grin is contagious and I giggle.

"What happened to the Mel I used to know? Did you kidnap her or what?" Tiny pink bows cover her white t-shirt. It looks so cute with her denim blue capris. Searching her face, I giggle again. No black eyeliner, only a little mascara, a hint of blue eyeshadow, and pink lipstick. I didn't expect this.

"Before you go all nuts on me, I am taking on a new lease on life. I cleaned out my closet and packed away most of my goth stuff. My mom is helping me out since she loved the makeover you did on me. She bought me some new clothes and make-up." Melody's grin lights up her face.

"No way, I can't friggin' believe it!" I tell her. "It is an awesome step in the right direction, Mel. Where's your necklace?"

Melody reaches inside the neck of her shirt and pulls out the chain with the pentagram dangling from it. Then she turns to me with a smirk. "I will never let this go. It's a symbol of my faith and represents the earth. You started the ball rolling, and I wanted to change my dark appearance for the best. It may help me forget Blaine and all his darkness." Mel looks down at her necklace and folds her fingers around the five-pointed star, then she holds it to her heart. "I need to be true to myself."

I pat her shoulder. "Good for you." Then, I stand up as I see my mother pulling into the parking lot in my peripheral. "Let's go."

The sun is high in the sky now, as we take the quick trip home. Mom turns off the car, and we follow her into the house. The garlic aroma hits us first. On the table sits a pizza from Pizza One®, some paper plates, and three cans of soda.

"Mrs. W, thanks so much. Pizza is my favorite!" Melody pulls my mom into a hug.

"I remembered," Mom replies.

We all sit at the table and dig into this wonderful lunch. My mom, she's all right. I appreciate her thoughtfulness. She winks at me and takes a bite.

Between bites, we make small talk. Mom asks about Mel's mother and about how they are doing in their new place. They discuss her new school and her new town. After we're done, we help clean up and put the food in the kitchen.

"Hey, Mom, is it okay if Melody sleeps over tonight? Her mother already said it was okay."

"Of course, honey." She looks over at Mel. "Mel, I love this new you. You are so beautiful!"

"Thanks!"

I lead the way up the stairs.

"Mel, come and sit on the bed. I have something important to tell you," I say, taking her backpack from her and tossing it on the floor near my desk. She lays her hoodie on top of the pack and hops on my bed.

Crossing her legs, Melody turns to me, awaiting the "talk". "Okay, what's going on?"

"I just want to clear the way. Please keep an open mind."

"Now you're scaring me," she replies.

I swallow and put it out there. "I don't know if you believe in spirits and visitations, but your father, being concerned about you, has visited me in my dreams several times. He has tried to guide me and the group to help change your karma by getting you away from Blaine."

Mel wrings her hands as she looks down at them. "I'll admit that I believe in ghosts and spirits, but why would my dad come to you?"

"Because he knows I can hear spirits and would get the job done. He also showed me one of your past lives and some events that happened. Billy and Blaine were also part of that lifetime. Me, too. We were all from the same Native American tribe. Blaine manipulated you in that lifetime to mess with Billy in order to create a rift between all the friends. Jimmy was there too. When you and Jimmy were young, you made a pact to love each other forever. But Blaine conned us all with his plan to breach that pact."

Melody smacks the comforter hard. "God, Rach, that's a lot to swallow. Do you believe all of this?"

"I know it to be true. I've seen the vision countless times, and truth be told, Jimmy has seen the same vision. We've compared our dreams and visions and they match. Blaine has put you on a downward spiral for several lifetimes." I search her eyes for any kind of acknowledgment.

Melody's eyes get all glassy. She grabs my hands. "This explains a lot of things," she says. "I sometimes dream of Jimmy, dressed in Native American garb, even though I did not know who he was. My heart goes all pitter-patter when this happens." She looks away for a second and says she thought she was going crazy. Then she swipes at her tears.

I grab her chin and force her attention my way. "So, do you believe me now? Do you trust me?"

"Yes, I do," the tears are streaming down her face now and I wrap her in a tight embrace. We stay locked together like this for several minutes to give her a chance to calm down.

Then I pull back. "Hey, we can meet up with Jimmy to sort this all out and figure out how we can fix your karma, if that is even possible. Blaine is gone, so that's the first step."

"Okay, I'd like that, if Jimmy is willing," she says.

I can see her eyes drift over to my desk, which is lined with crystals. I intended to capture my friend's interest with the shiny stones.

BINGO, it worked.

Chapter 30

CRYSTAL GRIDS

"A girl after my own heart. I simply love crystals; I see you do too," I admit to Melody.

"What a fantastic collection you have." Mel picks up and cradles my treasured quartz crystal in her fist. She closes her eyes, feeling the energy. "Wow, this stone is energized to the max. It's very powerful."

"That one is my favorite. You can use it as a wand, too. That crystal helped me find you the night of the Ball. It lit the way for me."

"How did you do that? Tell me more." Melody turns around to face me, still cupping the gemstone.

"Well, during our sessions, the Psychic Circle has been working with crystals and learning to empower them. That night, we put it to the test. We each brought our favorite rock with us—Blue Agate, Rose Quartz, Hematite, Amethyst, and Green Agate. My Quartz Crystal point boosted the other energies, and when combined, they helped to find you."

"That's amazing!" Melody's voice raises. "I'd love to know how to do that with the gang."

I pause for a moment, then I look at her. "Um... Mel, the group will not let you in. They still blame you for all the evil stuff that went on. Sorry." I put my hand on her arm. "But I can teach you, our friendship deserves a second chance."

"Too bad," she says. "A lot of bad things happened and for that, I'm so sorry. Blaine caused me to do some evil stuff. Thanks for the second chance. I promise to earn your trust again." Mel gives me a side hug.

I move the crystals to the bed and spread them across my comforter, trying to teach Melody about each crystal's energy and purpose. We practice charging them up and feeling what they can do.

"I've been reading about Crystal Grids and I want to try one with you if you are okay with it. What do you say?" I ask.

"Well, tell me what a grid is, then I'll decide."

"First, you select a geometric figure and draw it on a piece of paper, kind of like a pattern. Each geometric shape has a certain purpose. You pick the intent you want to work on and choose which crystals will help you zero in on your plan. Once you know your purpose, lay the stones on the points on that grid. The grids work with the combined energy of the crystals in a certain pattern."

"Okay, I'm in. Let's try it out. What did you have in mind?" Melody stands up and rubs her hands together.

I head over to my desk and pull out the top drawer, where I have print-outs of geometric shapes I found online. I leaf through them, select the pentagram shape, and place it on the desktop. "We should use the pentagram, since you are familiar with it. It's the perfect shape for releasing energy. I thought we would work on forgiveness and karmic issues."

"Sounds good to me." There's excitement in her voice.

"The crystals we choose vibrate at their own frequency and attract similar energy using the Law of

Attraction. Like energy attracts the same energy, so positive energy will attract positive energy."

"Good idea. It makes sense." Mel's face is beaming.

Grabbing a small velvet bag from the same drawer, I open it and allow the chosen stones to tumble out–1 Rose Quartz, 5 each of Green Calcites, Celestites, and Citrines. I pick up the Rose Quartz. "In the center, we place the focus stone. I choose Rose Quartz for unconditional love and forgiveness. That should be our focus. It will help mend our friendship."

Melody repositions the desk chair and sits down. "I like where this is going." I hand her the smooth pink stone, and she places it in the center of the Pentacle pattern.

I scoop up the 5 blue stones called Celestite. "These are the directional stones. Celestite helps to remove blockages and persistent thought patterns, which will also help us work with karmic issues." I place one at each of the 5 points of the pentagram map.

"Celestite is such a beautiful blue color. I think that's one of my favorites," says Melody as she runs her finger along the multiple smooth faces.

"Just a few more to go. I want to add Green Calcite as the Desire Stone. Desire stones help fine-tune or amplify the energy of your focus stone. Green Calcite absorbs the excess energy of anger, hurt, and bitterness. It stimulates the heart chakra for necessary forgiveness. It also promotes friendship, which is perfect for our purpose." I place the green stones at the 5 intersections of the lines.

"Wow, I'm blown away. You've learned a lot about grids in such a short time." Mel runs her hands across my shoulders.

"Thanks, but I'm not done yet. Last, Citrine releases emotional baggage and builds self-esteem." Gathering the five remaining yellow stones, I hand two to Mel, and I hold on to the last three. I take a Citrine and place it in between the first two Celestite stones.

Next, I continue with the others in my hand, while Mel places the last two.

I straighten up. "We need to write our intentions on a piece of paper and slide it under the focus stone. Once complete it, we must energize the grid." I produce a folded slip of paper and hand it to Mel.

She looks at me inquisitively.

"Go ahead, open it up," I say.

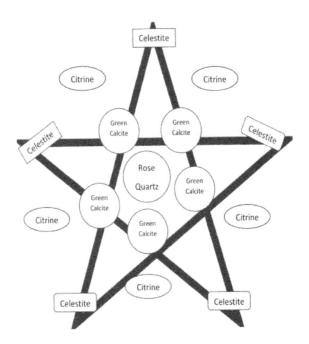

STONE PLACEMENT

Melody slowly unfolds the paper and reads our intention message aloud:

'Please allow us to release emotional blockages and stimulate our hearts for forgiveness. Allow us to repair our friendship, learn to trust again, and re-direct the course of karma.'

She folds it back up and places it underneath the Rose Quartz. Mel says, "Good to go. It's perfect." She claps her hands in a series of mini-claps, just like old times.

I put my hand in my best friend's free hand while we place our palms on the nearest crystals. We're concentrating on our intent message as we feel our energies flow through the stone layout and back to each other.

All the pieces are in position, so we'll see if this works.

Crossing my fingers.

Chapter 31

DESTINY UNFOLDS

The end of the week arrives in a flash. I can't believe we have one more week of school left. Melody and I have made plans to meet up at Jimmy's house. We need to figure out the destiny unfolding. I'm praying for a productive afternoon.

Jimmy opens up the door even before we ring the bell. "Hi guys," he says. "Come on in."

Melody's face lights up at his greeting. She walks around me and enters the house like she is on autopilot. I follow her.

"Hey Jimmy, you didn't tell the others about this little gathering, right?" I ask. "I don't want the group getting aggravated over us talking with the 'enemy' in private.

"Not a word." He displays the zipping-up lip motion.

"Good. None of them want to be involved. So, what they don't know won't hurt them." I smile.

Jimmy leads us to the back of the house after shutting the door behind us. Melody and I sink into the comfy navy-blue couch in the den. It brings back memories of when we rescued Mel the night of the Ball.

Jimmy moves over to the sliding doors and makes sure the lock is on, pulling the drapes closed. "My mom is at the grocery store. She'll be gone for a couple of hours. I thought we'd perform a past-life meditation together to find out if we all have the same vision. We can take it from there."

I grab Melody's hand and ask, "Are you cool with that, Mel?"

"Yes, let's do it," she says in a soft voice, as she flips her hair behind her ears.

Jimmy dims the lights and sits down on the couch next to Melody. "I have a copy of a meditation that Sofie gave me a while ago. It will help us with the regression." He puts the CD in the player and hits the play button.

"Okay, I remember this. Let's hold hands and listen to the instructions said over the Native American music," I say as I reach for Mel's hand, and she offers her other one to Jimmy. "Now we should lean back and close our eyes."

The soft melody fills the room with drums and flutes. Sofie's voice comes through over the music, asking us to set the scene by envisioning that we are Lakota Indians living in teepees. This should lead us to the same lifetime. Her voice pauses a moment, so we can see this in our minds. Jimmy hums to the music and Melody joins in, so I hum along too. It's addicting.

I feel my body relaxing, one muscle at a time. Melody's arm relaxes as her hand loosens up in mine. In my mind's eye, I view us sitting in a grass clearing, all cross-legged around a fire pit. Again, the fire's heat warms my body. Jimmy sits on a log next to me in front of the fire. Though Billy wasn't in the room where we started, I recognize him through the flames in this vision. An elder performs some sort of ceremony over the fire, spreading herbs and creating smoke.

In the background, a dark-haired girl crosses over toward a teepee behind her. Jimmy is watching this girl's every move with a huge smile. The mystery girl turns our way and throws Jimmy a kiss, continuing on her way. Although I have seen this a dozen times, I now realize it's our Melody without her dark makeup. We saw this part in our Past Life Regression session, which coincides with Jimmy's dreams.

The elder motions for Billy to follow the girl into the teepee. Meanwhile, my eyes are burning from all the smoke. As I blink, I notice Jimmy is being affected, too. We close our eyes instinctively, and when we open them, Jimmy and I are kneeling next to that teepee. He picks up the edge of the deer hide to peek inside. Just like in our prior visions, there is a movement under the deerskin blanket. That girl, Melody, is feverishly kissing Billy, who is kissing back. Mel looks at us over her shoulder with a sly grin and assaults Billy with another aggressive kiss. It's making me sick to view this again.

Suddenly, I turn to my right and notice the current-day Melody kneeling next to me with her tears threatening to fall, holding my hand tight. She has just witnessed her past self in action, and I'm sure it is a hard pill for her to swallow. Next, the vision morphs into a snippet of two 10-year-olds—Jimmy and Melody, promising to love each other forever. We witness the blood ritual they perform together, sealing their pact.

The vision turns to Melody in a constrictive bear hug with a different guy in the woods. She struggles to get free of his taut embrace that is restraining her, and screams, "You're hurting me!" Mel's legs and arms are flailing about.

We now know that he is the current-day Blaine. My blood is boiling. Then Blaine says, "She's all mine this time and her power is all mine. There is nothing you can do."

I am ready to lose it.

We can't change it since it's only a vision. But Jimmy shouts back, "Over my dead body!" With that, we snap back out of the meditation. All 3 of us are sitting in the den where we began, still holding hands. I glance over at Melody as she grabs both of Jimmy's hands and sobs hysterically. "I am so sorry," she cries between sobs. *I'm glad that Mel had the chance to see this whole thing herself in this meditation.*

Jimmy pulls her closer and wraps his arms around Mel as they rock back and forth together. "Don't worry, he's gone now and will never hurt you again. Over my dead body!" He moves back a bit, runs his hand through her hair, and wipes away her tears with his fingers. "You're going to be okay now." He places a gentle kiss across her lips and wraps her in a loving embrace.

"Aw, guys... you are making me cry," I say as the tears stream down my face. I get up for a group hug.

Chapter 32

SOULS LIKE US

"Karma is a law of the spiritual world. We are responsible for our actions and the intention of our actions. This responsibility exists within the context of an individual soul's relationship with God. When one deliberately disobeys the will of God, Karma is accrued." According to The Blog by Judith Johnson, www.huffpost.com.

It's the last day of school before summer vacation. I finally release a sigh of relief as I sit at our group's lunch table, waiting for the gang to come back from the food line, reflecting on the state of my life. I close my eyes for a moment. My world is relatively calm lately.

Amen! I shout from the mountaintop. My best friend, Melody, is back in my world. We have earned each other's trust again. I'm convinced she has turned over a new leaf, I mean permanently. And I am excited to say she has irrevocably found love. Melody and Jimmy are dating. They are head-over-heels in love with each other. She still is going to school in the next town, but every time I see them together in our town, they are locking lips. Mel has also kept the 'new look' going. No more gothic black attire; the makeup is lighter; she has a new lease on life, and I am so impressed.

Melody has made some amends with the group. The members of the Psychic Circle are talking to Melody again on social media. It's a step in the right direction. But she still is not welcome to attend our meetings. Time will tell—we'll see how it goes. Maybe in the future. Since she doesn't live in town anymore, my best friend visits me every other weekend, sometimes having sleepovers. Our group activities almost always involve our boyfriends, Jimmy and Billy. We double-date even though Billy still has his guard up. *Too much water under the bridge.*

Collectively, we've done our best to get Melody's karma back on track on a technicality—she was being controlled by Blaine the majority of the time. Her proud father still visits me from beyond and has confirmed this. Archangel Michael consulted with her father and reassured him they had broken the cycle of Blaine wanting Mel and her power.

Blaine has disappeared from her life and we are confident that he is gone once and for all.

As for the Psychic Circle, we try to meet once a month to work on our crystal knowledge and set up some crystal grids. We know from experience that crystal power is a real thing, and we are getting good at using it. Practice makes perfect. Our connection is deep-rooted and enduring. We are constantly practicing telepathy, meditation, and psychic development amongst us. Jasmine, Clarissa, Deanna, Sofie, Jimmy, Billy, and I will be friends forever, as we have quite a lasting bond. Who knows what the future holds for us? All that I know is that we will tackle it together because when we act as a whole, we can overcome any situation.

Billy and I are still going strong. I'm convinced that he's my soulmate. There is no doubt in my mind. He treats me like a queen and I love it. I primarily like that I can be myself around him, and my boyfriend agrees the feeling is mutual. We are closer now than ever before. And I especially love playing our little touching games when his mom goes out of town. LOL!

I glance down at the petite ring he recently gave me. It's a promise ring, a beautiful cubic zirconia band with three tiny stones. One day, he tells me, he will replace it with an engagement ring when we are ready for that stage of life. And I know deep down inside that I will marry this wonderful guy someday.

I peek over at Billy, now sitting next to me at the lunch table as he casually chats with our friends, and I feel a huge smile spreading across my face. *He's mine, all mine,* I think to myself.

Billy can sense my energy and hear my thoughts too, so he turns to face me. Billy's voice is in my head–*You're mine, all mine, too.* He gives me that famous smirk, then he gently covers my lips with his in a passionate kiss, right here in front of everyone.

Happy endings can happen in the real world, not just in fairy tales!

The End.

Thank you for Reading –

KARMA LIKE THIS
(The Psychic Circle Series – Book 3)

If you enjoyed this book, please consider leaving a quick review–just a sentence or two will do. You can leave a review at your point of purchase. It only takes a second. We appreciate your comments and reviews so much. It always helps the author and the book's rating.

Thank you for your help!

D. L. Cocchio

D. L. Cocchio

BIBLIOGRAPHY

Great Resources to Check Out

(They were all used in the writing of this book.)

1. Bradley, Jude & Chere Dastugue Coen. *Magic's in the Bag.* Woodbury, Minnesota (Llewellyn Publications) 2010. P.183-184.
2. Center for Inner Peace. Prayers of Protection. http://www.centerforinnerpeace.org
3. Dolfyn. *Crystal Wisdom, Spiritual Properties of Crystals and Gemstones.* Oakland, California. (Earthspirit Inc.) 1990-Third Printing.
4. Frazier, Karen. *An Introduction to Crystal Grids*. Emeryville, California. (Rockridge Press) 2019. p.136-137.
5. Kelmenson, Kalia. Spiritual Meaning of the Blood Moon. Spirituality &Health Magazine. https://www.spiritualityhealth.com/spiritual-meaning-of-the-blood-moon
6. Lambert, Mary. Crystal Energy. New York: Sterling Publishing Co, Inc., 2005.
7. Morrison, Dorothy. Everyday Magic. Minnesota: Llewellyn Publications, 2003.
8. Paranormal State, A&E. *Prayer of Protection.* http://www.aetv.com/paranormal-state
9. Permutt, Phillip. *The Book of Crystal Grids.* New York, NY (CICO Books 2017) an imprint of Ryland Peters + Small Ltd/London
10. Salem Live Ghost Hunt. The Travel Channel/Discovery Channel. http://www.travelchannel.com/shows/haunted-salem-live/episodes/1

D. L. Cocchio

Connect With the Author –

Social Media

~Where to contact the author -

Website: http://www.dlcocchio.webs.com

Amazon: www.amazon.com/author/dlcocchio

Facebook: www.facebook.com/debbiecocchio

Email: debbiecocchio@yahoo.com

Her books are available on...

Amazon Books, Amazon KDP, Barnes and Noble,

or you can ask for it at your local bookstore.

D. L. Cocchio

ABOUT THE AUTHOR

D. L. Cocchio is fascinated by all things mystical and magical. She has enjoyed writing stories since she was a child and is never seen without her Kindle. The author of five novels – *Be Careful What You Wish For, Magic By Moonlight, So You Wanna Read Tarot?* Including, The Psychic Circle Series Trilogy- *Souls Entwined, and Magic Like That, and Karma Like This.*

Cocchio has a degree in Psychology and in Education. Once an elementary school teacher, she also worked in the business world by day, and as an author by night. In her spare time, Cocchio enjoys ghost hunting with the Garden State Paranormal Society (G.S.P.S.), where she is one of the lead investigators. Debbie is currently retired, allowing herself the luxury to write more often when she is not watching her grandson. She lives in New Jersey with her husband, Gary.

D. L. Cocchio

BE SURE TO LOOK FOR OTHER BOOKS

IN THIS SERIES

 <u>Souls Entwined</u> – The Psychic Circle Series – Book 1

Sixteen-year-old Rachel's psychic world is shaken when Billy introduces her to telepathy and astral travel, awakening her desire for more spiritual adventure. She can't get enough. Together with a teenage shaman, a healer, a psychic, and a witch, they form "The Psychic Circle" to secretly explore the paranormal.

Romance blossoms between Rachel and Billy as they realize they have such a strong connection. Could Rachel possibly have found her soul mate? But when Rachel's best friend becomes jealous and causes issues using black magic, it can sabotage her chance at having the true love she's been yearning for.

Betrayed by her BFF, Rachel must decide if she should fight fire with fire using her own brand of magic, thus sacrificing what remains of their friendship in order to protect and pursue this obvious soul connection. All's fair in love and war, right?

D. L. Cocchio

 ## Magic Like That – The Psychic Circle Series – Book 2

Just when Rachel thought the drama was over and her 16-year-old psychic life was back to normal, her ex-best friend Melody resurfaces with her sights on Rachel's boyfriend, Billy. Melody will stop at nothing, delving deeper into the dark side of magic to get what she wants.

Trying to deal with the unwarranted vengeance targeted against her, Rachel knows she is not safe. But after catching Melody and Billy kissing and witnessing a secret binding ritual, Rachel is not sure whom she can trust anymore. So, when Rachel stumbles upon an old spell book in a locker, she enlists her Psychic Circle group to help beat Melody at her own game. Determined that nothing will disrupt the wonderful soul connection she has with Billy, Rachel must decide how far she will go to protect her soul mate, even if it means putting herself in grave danger.

D. L. Cocchio

Karma Like This – The Psychic Circle Series – Book 3

Under a paralyzing spell, things are looking grim for Rachel as she finds herself in quite a predicament. Her ex-best friend Melody has claimed retribution using black magic. Luckily, Rachel's strong telepathic connection with her boyfriend, Billy, saves the day when he brings the Psychic Circle group to help.

Dealing with Melody is not going to be as easy as they thought. She's breaking all the rules that could be cause for banishment. Rachel's visions have been intensifying and permeating her dreams with signs to help resolve 'the Melody situation'. Past Life Regression verifies her visions as the key to possibly altering the course of Karma.

The psychic war escalates at the Midsummer Night's Dream Costume Ball, where Rachel and Billy enlist Jimmy to help them turn this bad situation around. Can they change the course of Karma? Or is the saying true – 'Whatever will be, will be?'

OTHER BOOKS
by D. L. Cocchio

(Ask for them at your favorite bookstore, or online at
Amazon.com.)

The Psychic Circle Series (high school – adult)

The Psychic Circle ~ Souls Entwined – Book 1

Magic Like That – Book 2

Karma Like This – Book 3

The Amulet Series: (middle-school)

Be Careful What You Wish For – Book 1

Magic By Moonlight – Book 2

Non-Fiction: (Instructional Series – all ages)

So You Wanna Read Tarot?

D. L. Cocchio

KARMA LIKE THIS

Made in the USA
Middletown, DE
28 May 2023